HALLOWEEN NIGHT FEVER: END OF THE LONG WALK

By
Dan Graffeo

Aventine Press

The Street by H.P. Lovecraft was originally published as part of the collection, Dagon and Other Macabre Tales by Arkham House Publishers, P.O. Box 546, Sauk City, WI 53583. Used with permission.

Moss, J. Performed by Jim Henson -voice of Ernie. (1970). Rubber Duckie. Festival Attractions, Inc.

Marks, Johnny. (1949). Rudolph the Red-Nosed Reindeer. The Rudolph Company, L.P.

© 2009, Dan Graffeo
First Edition

Published by Aventine Press
750 State St. #319
San Diego CA, 92101

ISBN: 1-59330-577-X

Library of Congress Control Number: 2009921941
Library of Congress Cataloging-in-Publication Data
Halloween Night Fever: End Of The Long Walk

"There be those who say that things and places have souls and there be those who say they have not; I dare not say, myself, but I will tell of the Street."
—H.P. Lovecraft

ACKNOWLEDGMENTS

Halloween has always been my favorite night of the year. Those memories, however, wouldn't have been as fond without the following persons. My father, Paul, introduced me to the long walk (namely, the lengthy street I grew up on.) My mother, Janet, transformed me into Dracula, the Lone Ranger, and "Rowdy" Roddy Piper. My brother, Dean, showed me the fine art of tricking houses and mailboxes with shaving cream. My sister, Nicole, who didn't mind being Peter Criss when the neighborhood boys wanted to dress as *Kiss*. A special thanks goes to Jon and Erica McCahon, who have read all five *Halloween Night Fever* novels and will not reveal anything should a curious reader ask them. I must also thank Craig Cailler for helping me with the website and all my technological deficiencies. Finally, I can't thank my precious wife, Kim, enough. Her support with my Craft has been a firm foundation in my life, but there is something else that is more noteworthy. We proclaimed our love for each other on October 31, 2003. The magic on Halloween night is real. I'm proof of that.

This novel is for Courtney, Stephanie, and Derek. Thanks for letting me go trick-or-treating with you.

III

CHAPTER 1

Willy Hynes couldn't remember what it was that drew him to the orange light. He wasn't eager to zone in on the flickering because of boredom or even out of curiosity. The desire to find its source felt like instinct as his feet crackled through the dead leaves. It was a dark night. Willy was in the middle of the woods with no recollection of where he came from, where he was going, or what he would encounter be it the largest bogeyman or the smallest cricket. Thankfully, it was autumn and the mosquitoes had perished. Yet, other obstacles abound as he traveled the somber forest. Willy had run into a large spider web once and caught hemlock branches in the face twice. The sensations from the needles were more inconvenient than painful. It was a handful of these crimps that made Willy take his brown eyes away from the blinking orange light. It was the only light that gave shapes to the thick oaks and delicate elms that had digested him.

Willy came upon a calm river when he reached the forest's end. The river separated him from the orange light's origin, which seemed to come from an island on the other side. The river looked Canadian cold, despite the warm reflections of light in its tiny waves. There was a half-mile between him and the island. He didn't know what his next move should be. All he knew was that he had to get across somehow.

All he knew was the light.

He thought of stripping his clothes and diving in with hopes that the water wasn't as frigid as it appeared and of course, not drowning. He shed his *Oakland Raiders* jacket then took hold of his collared blue shirt. He almost buried his nose inside the fabric when he noticed a figure standing on the river in silhouette with the orange light.

It was a man with a strong physique. He had droopy jowls that made him look stern and battle-scarred. His hair was onyx black. His attire was a square piece of animal fur that covered his crotch. If Willy were to classify him by nationality, he would bet that the man was Native American. When Willy's eyes lowered, he saw that the Native American didn't stand on the water, but on the edge of a crude wooden boat.

The Native American motioned his hand.

Willy took a step forward, though he didn't know why.

The Native American turned his back and bent over. When he shifted back to Willy, he held an oar.

Willy's mind clouded with thoughts and questions as to whom this strange Indian was and why he offered Willy a ride across the river. What plans did he have for Willy when they arrive on the island? The Native American didn't appear armed and yet there was a force of some kind that embraced and penetrated him. Willy could feel it. It was a power that he had never felt in his thirteen years of being alive. It felt foreign, with a mix of danger and topped with a rush of unconditional excitement.

Willy put his jacket back on and got in the boat.

And the Native American paddled.

The ride was slow and neither individual spoke. For some reason, there was no necessity for verbal conversations. Willy, who was never at a loss for words, especially wisecracks, was as quiet as a blank canvas. He was positive that he could have come up with a few smart-alec remarks to the Native, like calling him "Tonto" or saying "How."

"Hey chief, how many payments have you got left on this yacht?"

Willy can picture himself blurting such a statement. Nevertheless, he kept to himself and watched as the island that held the orange glow branched out in every direction.

The Native ferryman struck his oar on the island's shore. He pulled hard as he shifted his weight and the boat as close to land as he could. Willy felt the boat's floor scrape against the wet gravel underneath. The island's outer core was populated with trees that seem to tickle the moonless sky and as black as a universe without stars. And somewhere in its heart was the flickering orange light.

The Native ferryman pointed his finger in the same direction that Willy was drawn to. Willy nodded in appreciation for the ride then dunked his black sneakers into the shallow waters. He sloshed his way to shore and then hurried into the woods to solve the glowing mystery.

He closed in on the orange glint as he pushed dozens of branches aside and crunched an uncountable amount of twigs and dried leaves wherever he stepped. For a second or two, he wished that he had removed his sneakers when he dipped his feet into the water. His socks were drenched and burbled every time he moved. Such petty burdens were forgotten when he found the orange light's source.

A massive bonfire stood before him.

African youths, most of them around nineteen-years-old, surrounded the bonfire. They stared at Willy as if he were the lead performer in a show they had waited for. Willy didn't recognize any of them, but the feeling of déjà vu teased his brain and encouraged him to keep guessing. He wanted to think that he was related to them somehow, yet he never recalled their presence in family photo albums nor reunions. Some of them looked as if they belonged in the 1960s, donned in bell-bottom pants, silk flowered shirts, and tassel vests. Others looked like slaves from the nineteenth century with their filthy shirts, torn pants, and straw hats. Most of them looked like they could pass today's dress code. All of them stood tall with proud expressions on their faces.

A warrior emerged from behind the flames. He approached Willy.

The dark-skinned warrior stood out from the rest because he resembled a comic book hero. He wore black with blue boots, gloves, belt, knee and elbow pads. A silver seven-pointed star was pinned on his right pectoral like a sheriff's badge. His cape, which was black on the outside and blue on the inside, hung down to his ankles. A blue raccoon-style mask kept the warrior's identity secret. Willy studied the warrior's chiseled chin and thick lips as he got closer. The warrior looked familiar like the others, yet Willy couldn't place a name or relation. The warrior's eyes were of no help either. Behind the mask were two pale slits instead of eyeballs. They shined like the blaze beside them.

"Don't be afraid, Willy," the warrior said, "you're with friends here."

"Who are you guys?" Willy said.

"Come."

Willy sauntered over to the warrior. They walked in a semi-circle to the other side of the bonfire where they came upon another Native American who was sitting down. This one was older than the ferryman was. He looked to be a hundred-years-old. His face was like red leather next to the fire. The countless wrinkles made it difficult to tell where his eyes and mouth were. A war bonnet made of hawk feathers rested on top of his head. Strands of thin white hair rested on his scrawny bare chest.

The warrior stood behind Willy. He placed his gloved hands on Willy's shoulders.

"Could anyone else be my colt?" he said.

The old native shaman raised his arm and placed the tips of his first two fingers on Willy's forehead. Willy felt a faint amount of electricity come from the old man's body to explore his. The shaman then took his fingers away from Willy's head and placed them in the center of his torso.

There was a pause. The shaman looked in deep thought. Willy didn't know what the ancient one was thinking, but it was important. Every fiber of his being told him that.

A smile drew on the shaman's face. He looked to the warrior and shook his head.

"I don't want to put him in danger," the warrior said.

The shaman's smile was still intact. He touched Willy's heart and then spread his arms out like an eagle to the shapeless sky.

"He is worthy?" the warrior said.

The shaman nodded.

"I still have my doubts," the warrior said. "If I accept him as my successor, he will be pushed harder than he's ever been pushed before. I will watch over him and protect him harder than I've ever watched and protected him before."

The shaman nodded. He reached from behind the log he sat on and pulled out a square piece of cloth that measured three inches by four inches. He extended the cloth to Willy and grunted. Willy accepted the shaman's gift and rubbed his thumb on the material. When he got a closer look at it, he discovered that it wasn't cotton or wool. It was a piece of animal skin. Willy didn't know what to make of it, but grinned anyway and nodded to the shaman. He folded the animal skin in half. He turned his head to the side and placed the fur in his jacket pocket.

When he attempted to address the shaman, he saw an extreme close up of three hawk feathers. They tapped his brow.

A bright flash was all Willy remembered before he woke up.

September 19

"All right everyone, can I have your attention, please?"

An iron fist from Mr. McDuff usually ruled Willy's fifth period gym class. If anyone stepped out of line or so much as giggled, burped, or crossed their eyes, detention would be given and not just one. Today, the class had reason to be at ease and act nutty. They had a substitute: a female substitute. She had long brown hair and bangs that covered some of the acne on her forehead. Her slim physique made many of the thirteen-year-old girls jealous. She held a basketball under her arm and placed her free hand on her hip.

"I'll bet she's got her own personal trainer," Lindsey Halloway muttered to her best friend, Ally Wedgeward.

"I'll bet she's had surgery," Ally whispered.

"Can I get your attention, please?" the substitute said as she began to dribble the basketball.

The class didn't respond. They talked amongst themselves as if she were a tourist on the street asking directions in a foreign language. Tommy DuValle, Joe Youngman, and Kyle Nunero debated what the greatest video game of all time was: *Grand Theft Auto: Vice City* or *Madden NFL '07* and if *Guitar Hero* counted as a video game. Christine Reilly, Tammy Wilowski, and Jenna Piaz sought each other's advice on what to wear for the October seventeenth dance. Willy and his friends, Randy and Wes Garland, talked about the odds that the *New England Patriots* had for the *Super Bowl*. Erin O'Rainly insisted to Heather Cludessica that she didn't care what the consequences were for not changing for gym. She had a piano recital after school and she didn't have time to change out of her black dress and get sweaty.

"Can I get your attention, class?" the substitute said.

The talking got louder. There was even laughter. A "whatever" came out of someone's mouth.

The substitute dribbled the ball faster. When it looked like an orange blur, she threw it at the wall. The basketball was more like a cannon ball. It flew between Wes Garland and Willy's faces and missed them by inches as it struck the wall with a sound that echoed across the gymnasium.

Two or three girls yelped after they heard the impact.

The class hushed and turned their attention to the substitute, who had caught the ball that bounced back to her. Willy examined the white concrete wall between him and Wes Garland and searched for any kind of damage. If damage was measured by sound, a hole the size of a big screen TV should have been made. The wall was still intact.

"Oh good, I got your attention," the substitute said. "I was hoping to get started."

"Jeez, lady," Tommy DuValle said, "is it that time of the month?"

"Care to find out?" the substitute said.

"Not really," Tommy said.

"As you can see, Mr. McDuff is not here. My name is Miss Daniels and I'll be taking over for today," the substitute said. "According to his schedule, you guys are supposed to be playing basketball today."

"Uh, excuse me?" Erin O'Rainly said, "I can't play today. I'm dressed up."

"And you are?" Miss Daniels said, though to Erin it sounded more like an interrogation.

"Mr. McDuff and I have an understanding," Erin O' Rainly said. "If I don't want to change, I don't have to."

Miss Daniels knelt down and picked up her clipboard. After a quick glance, she turned back to her protestor. "You're Erin, aren't you?"

"Yeah," Erin said, "why?'

"Mr. McDuff left a note saying that an Erin O'Rainly will probably say that she can't participate, and if she does, I'm to remind her that this'll be her second zero. I had Mr. McDuff when I was thirteen too. Wasn't it his policy to flunk a student if they got more than four zeroes? You're gonna be working on your second and it's not even October yet."

Erin had no reply. She kicked off her black flats, folded her arms, and waited for the next order.

Miss Daniels smirked. "That's the spirit. Anyone else got a situation that needs to be handled?"

Joe Youngman stepped forward. He chewed bubble gum and offered his best grin.

"Yeah, I can't play," he said.

"Why not?" Miss Daniels said.

"I recently recovered from kidney surgery," Joe said. "Doc says I can't do any physical activity for four months. Too bad too. I love basketball."

"Where are your kidneys?" Miss Daniels said.

The sarcasm on Joe's face faded. He patted his stomach.

"Nice try," Miss Daniels said. She shoved the ball to him. Joe caught it like a normal, healthy junior high student.

"Let's see," Miss Daniels said, "we got one, two, three, four, five, six boys."

She pointed to Randy and Wes Garland as well as Willy.

"You three are the shirt team," she said. "The rest of you are the skin team."

As Tommy DuValle, Joe Youngman, and Kyle Nunero shed their shirts, Miss Daniels turned to the girls.

"One, two, three, four, five," she said, "not enough for a fair game."

"I could step out," Erin O'Rainly said.

"But then you'd miss out on all the fun," Miss Daniels said. "Go to the gym closet and bring out the barrel of balls. All you guys have to do is dribble and shoot and pretend you're really into the game. Fair enough?"

"Fine," Erin said.

Miss Cindy Daniels remembered her days of being thirteen. It was five years ago. She had been brash, arrogant, cared only about her boyfriend, Tim, and being a cheerleader for the *Boston Celtics*. Somewhere down the line, she had changed her mind as much as she changed boyfriends. Tim was yesterday's news and it was onto Brian, then Jimmy…then it was Dylan. Her interests shifted from being a professional cheerleader to a professional tennis player. Today, she settled for stability. She had been seeing a guy name Chris Tollen for the past five months. Her future ambition was to become a junior high gym teacher.

"Here we go," she said and threw the basketball in the air. Willy and Kyle Nunero both jumped for it, but it was Kyle who slapped the ball to his teammates and logically so. Kyle was at least four inches taller than Willy was.

Willy noticed how Miss Daniels kept an eye on him throughout the game. She looked at him as if he were a frog to be dissected and studied. Her stares persisted for minutes at a time and blinked away only when Erin O'Rainly asked if she could get a drink at the water fountain and when Jenna Piaz begged to go to the nurse. Miss Daniels acknowledged their presence and sent them away, then zoned in on Willy again. By the time there were ten minutes of class left, Willy was freaked out to the point where he failed to catch the ball and it smacked him in the stomach.

Willy clutched his gut and gasped for air.

"Come on, Hynes," Miss Daniels said while clapping, "shake it off."

Miss Daniels's words of encouragement hardly helped. Willy missed every time he shot for the basket. He always hit the rim.

Miss Daniels blew her whistle. "All right, go change!"

Tommy DuValle and Joe Youngman strutted past Willy.

"I thought the white guys were supposed to be lousy at basketball," Joe said.

Tommy laughed.

Willy repeatedly shrugged his shoulders and slapped his knee as he mocked them with his phony chuckle. As he was ready to follow them into the boy's locker room, he heard Miss Daniels.

"Willy?"

He turned around. Sweat tumbled down his brown skin as he waited for her additional comments.

"I hope you weren't tweaked out too much," she said, while picking up one of the basketballs. "You know, with me throwing the ball close to your face and my staring at you and b-b-bah."

"It's gonna take a little more than you to intimidate me," Willy said. "So what was the deal with all that?"

"With all what?" Miss Daniels said.

"The staring," Willy said. "You got a thing for me or somethin'?"

"No," Miss Daniels laughed. "I was just noticing your shooting style. It's very raw and unfocused."

"Meaning what?"

"Meaning next time, stare at the middle of the hoop," Miss Daniels dribbled one of the basketballs, "then let the ball roll off your fingers."

She threw the ball. It spun in the air and made a "swish" sound as it went through the hoop. She jogged up the court and swiped the ball before it made a second bounce.

She passed the ball to Willy. "Five seconds on the clock."

Willy couldn't hide his grin. He dribbled the ball and stared at the middle of the hoop. He let the ball roll off his fingers when he hurled it. The ball made a "swish" sound as it plummeted through the hoop.

"Nice job," Miss Daniels said and caught the rebound.

"Yeah, thanks," Willy said. "See ya around, aaaright?

CHAPTER 3

Willy hadn't realized how hot it was until he got off the air-conditioned bus and walked down Woodland Avenue towards his house. Bus number four roared back to life and rolled away. It left behind an obnoxious amount of white exhaust fumes. Willy held his breath and swatted away the carbon monoxide with his free hand. The buses, as far as he could tell, were the biggest pollution problems in town. Not that he really cared. As long as they got him from A to B, he wasn't going to give it much thought. All he wanted now was to go home, put on a pair of shorts, and drink a tall glass of *Coke*.

His shadow walked to the left of him as the unmerciful sun baked his right side. Willy re-gripped his books that were slipping from under his arm. This was his time to observe the suburban environment he lived in for the last few years. The trees were almost bare and the leaves that held onto their branches were brown and fragile. The next strong wind that came along would probably knock most of them off, but a few always managed to stick to their territory. The leaves that are driven off will land and scatter on lawns of Woodland Avenue's finest neighbors. Mr. McCorman will be out there first thing tomorrow morning to rake them up, while Mrs. McCorman busied herself with her sunflowers. Then there were persons like the Trolley's and the Hatfield's, who raked up their leaves in a big pile so their kids could get a running start and jump into it. After the fun, they will put the crinkled tree garments into a large orange trash bag that has the face of a jack o'lantern on the front of it. They will display it for Halloween and probably until the first snowfall. Then you had neighbors like the Plahtimere's who let the leaves pile on their property until one can't find a trace of grass anywhere.

Most of the birds had begun their trip down south with the exception of the owls and crows whose squawks were heard from streets beyond as they puttered across the yards and plucked out worms and any insect they laid eyes on. Willy didn't mind the crows because they were proof that the town had signs of life.

Welcome to Sleepy Owl, Connecticut, population 4,292, home of the Sleepy Owl Tomahawks football team and Jay Sassacus, the owner of the *Pequot Casino* in Hartford. Sleepy Owl has a slow-paced, friendly community. Its land is made up of forests, brooks, open fields, and Raven River, which provides a boundary between Sleepy Owl and its neighboring town, Donovan's Grove. Raven River also flows into Lake Black Feather, a popular sight for bass fishing and a history lover's dream because pirate artifacts had been found at its murky bottoms.

Willy didn't care for the town all that much.

He got along with almost everyone he met and made the honor roll twice in the last three years. There was never any trouble with the law and the thought of trying alcohol or drugs didn't interest him. With the exception of a few detentions for some wisecracks, Willy was as clean-cut, polite, and hard working as the next kid.

And yet something inside of him wanted go wild and bask in adventure.

The suburban life wasn't for him. Willy always dreamed of getting a job in New York or playing for the *Raiders* in Oakland among the glitter and bright lights of the big cities. He yearned to live in a place where he could be surrounded by exciting persons and see famous landmarks that he's only read about in books and seen on the Internet: places like the Empire State Building or the Statue of Liberty or the Hollywood sign or Mann's Chinese theatre. Unfortunately for Willy, whenever he expressed his interest in the fast lane, his father, Marvin Hynes, gave his speech of how he grew up poor in Boston and worked hard so that Willy could live in a safe place like Sleepy Owl. The closest Willy had come to such places after age five was on vacation with his parents and his big brother, Mike, before he died. Together, the Hynes's got a breath-taking view of Las Vegas in Nevada and looked down from the Sears Tower in Chicago. Willy remembered the excitement he felt when he saw persons from all walks of life trying to make it big. He remembered all the places to go and all the things to do. In the cities, he could eat at fancy restaurants that had bathroom attendants or go see a rock concert at the plazas or watch a football game at the stadiums. He could spend hours just walking the streets and wonder what kind of adventures he could get into.

Then he came home to Sleepy Owl. A town where the most exciting thing that happened was when the general store got the newest edition of *Sports Illustrated* or *Ghost Rider*, his favorite comic book.

CHAPTER
4

A s Willy approached the Takahoshi home, he saw Marty Takahoshi, who was two years old than he was. Marty sat on the rocking chair under his front porch. He adjusted his acoustic guitar and pushed his dark glasses to the top of his nose. He cleared his throat and readied the clip in hand. Willy heard traces of the opening melody and identified it as *Sister Hazel*'s song, "All for you."

Marty guessed that he had struck the next chord too hard and held his clip too loose. The clip freed itself from Marty's thumb and finger and fell onto the deck. It made a faint tinkle when it landed.

"Aw, great," Marty said. He felt along his chest for the strap. It didn't take long for him to recognize the seatbelt-like fabric as he pulled it over his head. He then reached for the guitar's neck and placed the instrument off to the side. Before he could bend over to search for his clip, he heard a familiar voice.

"Hey, Marty."

"Hey, Willy."

Willy trot up Marty's walkway. "What're you up to?"

"Oh, just practicing," Marty said. "How about yourself?"

"Nothing really. Are you watching *Saturday Night Live* tomorrow night? *U2* is playing."

"Wouldn't miss it. Who's hosting?"

"I have no clue. Did you see it last week when Martin Short hosted?"

"Yeah, it wasn't bad," said Marty, "of course I was a little disappointed that he didn't do his *Ed Grimley* character. I was kinda' looking forward to it. Compared to the classic sketches, everything else blows."

"That ain't true," Willy said.

"Yes, it is," Marty said. "Look at all the talented guys that came out of that show. You got Bill Murray, Mike Myers, Chris Farley, Chevy Chase…"

"Chris Farley is dead," said Willy, "and Chevy Chase doesn't count."

"What do you mean 'he doesn't count?'" Marty said.

"Wasn't he only there for a year?"

"I think that still counts."

"I think your taste in comedians suck."

"Whatever," said Marty. "Now get down there and get my clip."

Willy went up the three steps that separated the Takahoshi home from their lawn. He kneeled down next to Marty to view the deck. The black guitar clip stuck out amongst the sorrel-colored planks as it laid a foot or so away from a ceramic pot that contained a Japanese blue iris past its prime. Willy pinched the clip and held it up to Marty's chest area.

"Here you are," Willy said, "it's right near your—"

"I know," Marty said and took the clip out of Willy's hand. "Thanks. So what's up for the weekend?"

"Same old, same old," Willy said. "Me and Vince will do something and then I'll probably hang out with Daryl. You?"

"Band practice," Marty said. "I think my grandparents are coming up on Sunday. We'll probably go apple or pumpkin picking."

"Apple picking with the grandparents," Willy said. "How does your heart stand the excitement?"

"Believe me, this time of the year, I get all the excitement I can handle."

"Yeah, I can tell." Willy said and got up from his knees, "I'll catch ya later. Why don't you play something with a little soul?"

"I'll consider it," Marty said. "Pleasant dreams."

Willy wasn't sure what to make of Marty's comment.

"Yeah, aaaright," he said. "Pleasant dreams to you too."

Marty resumed his guitar practice as he strummed out the rest of "All for you," while Willy walked towards the end of Woodland Avenue to his house.

A week later, the weather had morphed from July hot to normal autumn temperatures. Willy had no need to wear his *Oakland Raiders* jacket until Friday night, September twenty-sixth, when his close friend, Vince Thomason, came by as he did every weekend to take Willy out. Vince was six years older than Willy was. When they first met, neither was impressed with the other and they had no idea that they would create a brother-like relationship. They met through Willy's late older brother, Mike, who was the same age as Vince. Vince and Mike became friends when the Hynes' first moved to the area eight years ago. At Sleepy Owl Elementary School, eleven-year-old Vince Thomason approached Mike Hynes.

"Name's Vince," he said. "How's it going?"

Mike smiled. "Hey, what's up?"

"Got a name?" Vince said.

"Mike."

"A few of us are getting a kickball game together at recess," Vince said. "You want in?"

"Yeah," Mike said, "yeah that sounds good."

From that moment on, Mike and Vince were inseparable. They always played football or hockey or just sat around and talked about whatever came to mind. Then one day, when Willy was five and watching *Spider-Man* on television, Mike came into the room with Vince behind him.

"Willy, I want you to meet my friend, Vince," Mike said.

Vince waved at Willy.

"Hi," Willy said and refocused on what the web-slinger had in store for *Dr. Octopus.*

Willy had seen Vince come over countless times after that. Over the years, Vince and Mike got braces put on and taken off, went on double dates, and joined the Sleepy Owl Tomahawks track team. All this time, neither Vince nor Willy ever said more than a couple of sentences to each other: mostly "excuse me."

Four years ago, tragedy struck when Mike was diagnosed with cancer and it spread through his body. When he was admitted to Hartford Hospital, Vince and Willy began to truly talk for the first time. They confessed of how scared they were of losing Mike. Vince tried his best to keep Willy's spirits up. When they didn't visit Mike, they played catch and went out for pizza. No matter how hard Vince tried, however, he couldn't prevent the inevitable. Mike Hynes died in his sleep months later. At the wake, Vince kneeled next to Mike's coffin and promised his friend that he would look after Willy. Since then, Vince had put one night a week aside for Willy while managing to graduate high school and get a job as an auto mechanic at *Murray's Garage*.

Tonight, they will get together and see the latest Adam Sandler movie. Willy exited his bedroom and went down the stairs to the family room. Marvin Hynes sat in his easy chair and read the *Sleepy Owl Times*, while Shayla Hynes, Willy's mother, sat on the couch and watched the evening news.

"Did you hear Vince's horn?" Willy said.

"No," said Shayla, "not yet. So where are you guys going tonight?"

"Movies," Willy said and then turned to his father.

The *Sleepy Owl Times* shielded Marvin from everyone.

Shayla turned to her husband as well and waited for him to put his paper down.

He didn't. Marvin kept reading, ignoring the pause that took hold of the room. He knew what was coming.

"Marvin," Shayla said and laughed, "give the boy some money."

The *Sleepy Owl Times* folded over. Marvin lowered his head and stared at his wife without the use of his thick glasses that rested on the edge of his nose. He adjusted his body and pulled out his wallet from his back pocket. He pulled out a dollar and extended it to Willy.

"Very funny, Marvin," Shayla said.

"Come on, Dad," Willy said, "Vince is gonna be here any minute."

"Will it help if I gave you another dollar?" Marvin said.

"It would help if you gave me a hundred," Willy said.

"Don't count on it, mister," Marvin traded the one-dollar bill in his hand for a ten. "Will this do?"

"Yeah, thanks." Willy took the money, "I could use some change though."

"I can't help you out there," Marvin said. "I spent my last dime on the parking meters."

"Dad, get up."

"Why?"

"Just get up," Willy said, "it'll only take a second."

Marvin sighed. He placed his newspaper on the coffee table next to him. He gave a low groan as he rose up from his easy chair. "What is it?"

Willy walked over to the chair and reached between the cushions. A high-pitched jingle was heard. Willy's fist came up with several coins.

Shayla laughed.

"You can sit now," Willy said.

Marvin bent over and took a closer look at his easy chair.

"Well I'll be," he said. "I should check in there more often. How long have you known about this?"

"Long enough," Willy said. He heard Vince's car horn. "I gotta go. Be back at eleven."

CHAPTER 6

"What's up?" Willy said as he got into the blue Mercury Sable.

"Ah, the usual," Vince Thomason said. "Working and what not."

Willy slammed the passenger side door. Vince pulled out of the driveway and drove down Woodland Avenue. The car's interior was so dark that Willy only saw a silhouette of Vince's head. Willy also detected a musty scent despite several pine car fresheners that hung from the rear view mirror.

"So what should we eat tonight?" Willy said.

"I'm in the mood for a little *Taco Bell*," Vince said. "Sound good to you?"

"Yeah, it does," Willy said, "but if it's too crowded, how about we go to the mall and eat? There's a CD I wanna get and I wanna see if they got any decent Halloween masks in. I'd be killing two birds with one stone."

"You made plans for Halloween already?" Vince said as he drove up to the end of Woodland Avenue and took a left onto Jenkins Avenue.

"Naw, not really," Willy said. "I figured I'll just get some bad-lookin' mask and do a little shaving cream activity. Maybe soap a couple of windows."

"Well that's definitely an option," Vince said. "What's the matter? You getting too old for trick-or-treating?"

"What do you think?" Willy said.

"I think you'd look adorable as *Boots*," Vince said.

Willy was five when he saw *Boots,* the monkey from the *Dora the Explorer* cartoon for the first time. He always told Vince and his folks that he wanted to be like *Boots*. He even begged his mother to buy him a *Boots* mask on Halloween. Less than a year later, he changed his mind—big time.

"Kiss mine," Willy said.

Vince snickered.

"Kiss mine," Willy sang louder.

"Sorry, sorry," Vince said as he came to a fork in the road. Usually, they kept to the left and ended up on Sleepy Owl's Main Street where the theatre was about eight miles away. This time, to Willy's surprise, Vince turned right onto Enfield Street.

"Yo, ain't we going to the show?"

"Yeah," Vince said.

"Well scuse me, Sherlock," Willy said, "but you just pulled a Stevie Wonder and took the wrong turn."

"I know where I'm going," Vince said. "We just got to make a little stop first."

"Where?"

"Huford House."

"No seriously, where?"

"Huford House."

"Vince, I ain't playin' with you. Where are we stopping?"

"Huford House."

Huford House was Sleepy Owl's claim to paranormal fame. It was a colonial style ramshackle mansion riddled with ghosts. Built in 1702 by Jeremiah Huford, a wealthy Dutch settler, Huford House was the sight of numerous balls and with the exception of a few Pequot Indians, was exclusive to the rich. That changed on Halloween night in 1757 when a bunch of persons, including Huford himself, were murdered. Since then, the residence has been the sight of many psychic investigations and supermarket tabloid papers. All of them claimed that the spirits of the 1757 Halloween massacre haunt the place. A few families tried to move in over the last two-hundred years. All of them left the house screaming within two weeks. After six exorcisms, Huford House still held its ground on being the habitat for the hereafter. The living had abandoned the home since 1913, but supernatural activity was still reported.

And Willy was heading for it.

He tried to keep calm and thought that perhaps Vince was pulling a prank on him. Yet, they were on Enfield Street and if they keep driving,

Baykok Avenue will be on the right. Huford House's address is 112
Baykok Avenue.

"Why would we go to Huford House?" Willy said.

"You'll see," Vince said.

"We ain't allowed on that property."

"Yes, we are." Vince flicked on his right blinker. They turned onto
Baykok Avenue. The numbers on the houses were in the teens.

"No, we're not!" Willy said, "And even if we were, why would you
go there? We got no business going there. Even the biggest jackass in
town knows not to go near there!"

"On the contrary," Vince said, "we have every business to be
there."

The numbers on the houses reached the one-hundreds. Willy was
frightened enough to consider opening the passenger door and jumping
out. Vince was usually passive, but remaining poker-faced while
meddling with the dead was enough for Willy to know that something
was wrong. Unfortunately, the Mercury Sable was going too fast for
Willy to make such a risky move.

Vince pushed on the brakes and put his car in park.

Willy looked past Vince's dark figure and gazed upon Huford
House, Sleepy Owl's edifice of fear. The waxing moon gave little light
to the surroundings. Vince got out of his vehicle and circled over to the
passenger side. He opened the passenger door as if he were on a date
and watched the understandable look of horror on Willy's face.

"Okay Vince," Willy said, "you had your fun. I'm scared out of my
wits, aaaright? I'll admit it, I'll put it in writing and I'll even broadcast
it. Now what say we get out'a here?"

"Trust me," Vince said.

"What do you mean 'trust you'? Trust you with what?"

Vince didn't answer. He started to walk up the hill toward the light-
deprived mansion. The only sounds came from the crunching of dead
leaves beneath his feet.

"Where are you going?" Willy said.

Vince closed in on Huford House with every step.

"Vince, you got three seconds!" Willy said as he got out of the car,
"If you don't tell me what's going on, I'm gonna book it up the street as
fast as I can! One….two…"

The walking stopped, but Vince didn't turn around.

"Willy, look in your right jacket pocket."

Silence occurred in Willy's reaction as he wondered what to think of Vince's remark: look in the right jacket pocket.

Willy slid his hand in his *Oakland Raider*'s right pocket.

He felt something furry. He remembered. But it couldn't be. How is it possible? Willy pulled out a square piece of animal fur, three inches by four inches.

The dream of the ferrymen and the Native American shaman barged out of his mind's deepest regions and collided with his consciousness with an impact that sent a shock wave up his backbone and erected the hair on the back of his neck.

Willy uttered a nervous snicker as his thumb rubbed the brown fibers.

"No," he muttered. "N-n-n-n-n-no."

The *right* pocket, Vince had said.

Willy sat on the passenger's side while Vince drove. There was no way Vince could have slipped something into Willy's pocket without Willy knowing it.

"It's caribou," Vince still gazed at Huford House. "The Pequot Indians used to wear their furs when they settled in this area thousands of years ago."

Willy was flabbergasted. "How did you know?"

"An old Native American man gave it to you in a dream, didn't he?"

"How could you have known?" Willy said, "I never even told anyone anything about—"

"Because I was there," Vince said and about-faced.

Willy walked up the hill, staring at Vince. Vince was wearing a raccoon-style mask. The mask was blue. Two white slits shined where his eyes should have been.

Willy lost his voice, like in the dream, as well as the instinct that told him when he should be scared or not. Vince had never hurt him in the past, but does past behavior apply now? Willy's jaw dropped so low that his chin was almost below his neck. He wanted the million questions in his mind answered, but nothing came out except babbling.

"I...I-I. How? I mean, I...W-What do you..?"

"Believe me when I say that I know exactly what you're feeling right now." Vince peeled off his mask. The pale slits were gone and his brown eyes were back. "Now close my door, shut your mouth, and follow me."

Huford House got creepier with every step Willy took. The only distinguished features that he noticed were the boarded up windows on the first floor, the tired shutters, the roof, the door, and the two unused porch light cases on both sides of it. The rest of it was pitch black and gave the illusion that whoever entered the house would endlessly float in limbo. The titanic oak tree to the right looked like a blot of spilled ink. Its branches were streams of darkness as they twisted and zigzagged to the sky, which left shadows on the yard's moonlit areas. Willy heard the stairs' agonized cry as he treaded on them. He felt ready to faint.

Vince walked across the porch and tried the door.

The entrance pushed open with a loud and extended whine that sounded like the entire house would collapse if the door opened any wider. As Willy expected, the inside was shrouded in darkness. A putrid stench escaped the catacomb and mingled with the suburban fresh air.

"I thought this place would be locked," Willy said.

"It is to those who don't belong here," Vince said. "We do. Let's go."

Vince stepped inside. The floor planks growled.

Willy took a deep breath. He crossed the threshold. He looked around the hallway, but his eyes hadn't adjusted to the dark. He viewed something shimmering on the ceiling and guessed that it was probably a crystal chandelier. He took a few steps forward and got on his tiptoes to take a closer look.

The door behind him slammed. He yelped.

Then the room lit up and gave the atmosphere a tangerine color. The candles on the walls, the tables, and bureaus had ignited by themselves. Willy screamed and charged for the door.

"Where are you going?" Vince said.

"GET ME OUT'A HERE!" Willy tugged on the doorknob.

"I told you that you don't have anything to worry about," Vince said. "Now come on. We got to go in the basement and talk."

Willy took his clammy hands off the doorknob and faced Vince. Cold sweat tumbled down his brow and armpits.

"What going on here!" he said. "Why are you so calm! Do you have any idea where we are! Have you forgotten all the things we've heard about this place!"

"Let's go down to the basement," Vince said. "Everything will be explained in the basement."

"I ain't going down no basement! You can explain it all right here, right now!"

"See you in the basement," Vince said. He walked out of the hallway and into the kitchen.

"Vince?"

Willy was being ignored now. His lifelong friend went into the kitchen and turned to his left. A door stood before him. He gave Willy a smile and wink, opened the door, and disappeared into the next room. Loud and hollow thumps echoed across the hallway as Vince made his way down the stairs. Willy wanted to stay in the hallway and focus on how to leave Huford House. Caribou skin or not, this place was known for its violent haunting and there was nothing that Vince could have told him here that he couldn't have told him at home.

Willy tried for the door again, but it was still locked. When he turned around to face the kitchen, he gasped.

A man wearing a powdered white wig and dressed in clothes that Willy guessed was from the 1700s stared at him. The man had come from nowhere, but what freaked Willy out was that he, Willy, was able see right through him. That left one explanation of what the man truly was. Willy flattened his back against the door and spread his arms as if he was a cornered wild animal that knew the end was near. The apparition tilted his head and then walked through the closest wall.

Huford House's front door was assaulted again. Willy yanked on the doorknob. He kicked at it and prayed that the lock would give in. It didn't. After that failure, Willy attempted to break the door down. He slammed his shoulder into the wood until he nearly lost the feeling in his arm.

Vince!" Willy said, "Vince! Wait up!"

He ran faster than any track star at Sleepy Owl High School. Willy darted across the hallway, into the kitchen, and through the basement arch. As he descended the stairs, he noticed that dozens of white candles were lit up on the basement's left side. Bookshelves coated with hundred-year-old dust filled up most of the walls. Antique furniture occupied the floor. The basement itself wasn't as chilly as he thought it would be. The candlelight gave it an almost tranquil atmosphere. The persons he saw sitting in the chairs and couches were, thankfully, alive.

Vince stood against the left wall. His arm rested on one of the bookshelves. His expression was welcoming, but serious. On the couch was Marty Takahoshi, cane in hand. He smiled and thought about how scared he was when it was his time to know the reason for visiting Huford House. Next to him was Jessey Sassacus, one of the last full-blooded Pequots and the richest girl in town, thanks to her father's ownership of the *Pequot Casino* in Hartford. Her deep black hair was woven into a braided ponytail. She wore a silver necklace with a turquoise in the center and a long dress with moccasin shoes. Willy remembered her when they went to Sleepy Owl Junior High School last year, but she was now fourteen and a freshman in high school. She had always kept to herself and spent most of her time with her face in a book. The friends he saw her with were few.

On the chair next to the couch was an overweight guy that Willy had seen around town every now and again, mostly at local football games. Willy was sure that he played for the Sleepy Owl Tomahawks, or at least used to. Willy hadn't seen him play this year and assumed that the guy was now in college. Bill—that was his name. Bill something. Bill leaned back, folded his hands, and placed them behind his head, letting them rest in his dirty blond hair. Next to Bill was a more familiar face: the face of a young woman with minor acne, but still pretty. She was eighteen with long brown hair and blue eyes.

"Your shooting got any better?" she said.

Was it her? It was, wasn't it? The crazy substitute from his gym class last week: the one that nearly took his head off with a basketball.

"Miss Daniels?"

"We're not in school now," she said. "You can call me 'Cindy.'"

Willy turned to Vince and folded his arms. "Aaaright, does someone want to tell me what this is all about?"

"You ever wonder where Halloween came from?" Vince said.

"Never thought much of it," Willy said. "It's a fun little holiday where you can get candy and dress up in a costume…but you're gonna tell me that there's more to it than that, aren't you?"

"More than you know," Marty Takahoshi said, "more than you know."

"According to the ancient Druids and Celts, Halloween was a time where the veil between our world and the supernatural world was at its thinnest," said Vince, "and on that night, the spirits of the dead were allowed to walk with the living."

"So?" Willy said.

"So the Pequot Indians also recorded in their history a night where the supernatural roamed the Earth," Vince said. "Many of these supernaturals were good and only wished to visit relatives and participate in the festivals. Some, however, were evil and around 7000 B.C., the Pequots formed groups called the Pniese, who maintained order every October thirty-first, helping the good and battling the evil."

"What does this have to do with me?"

"We all had the dream you had. You follow the orange light, a ferryman takes you to an island, and a Native American shaman looks you over and nods. Then he gives you a piece of caribou skin."

"Yeah, that's right," Willy said. He took out the piece of fur from his pocket, "So what's the deal with this then?"

"The caribou skin is a reminder of our history." It was Jessey Sassacus who spoke, "We wear it as a patch on our uniforms as a sign of respect to the great warriors of the past."

"Uniforms?" Willy said.

"Yeah, you see for centuries, the Pequots and the supernaturals had a mutual understanding," Vince said. "Then in 1614, a Dutch settler named Adriaen Block became the first white settler in Connecticut. Others soon followed and on Halloween, the white settlers were shocked to see the supernaturals roaming the land. They believed that all of them were evil and attacked. Many supernaturals and Pequots were killed that night. A year later, the Irish tradition of Halloween was introduced and people began wearing costumes, which made it difficult to distinguish between the living and the dead. The Pequots also adopted this custom. At the same time, the Pequots convinced the white settlers that the supernaturals would never return and as a result, they now had two tasks: one, to keep the peace and two, to keep the supernaturals a secret to the white men."

Willy let out a slight chuckle and shrugged his shoulders.

"I'm only going to say this one more time," he said. "Just what does any of this got to do with me?"

"Well—" Vince said.

"Ah-ah!" Willy held up a finger, "I don't wanna hear no more crazy mumbo-jumbo ghost and goblins stories. I just want my question answered."

"Real patient isn't he?" Bill said, "This is your Colt, Vince? Good luck."

"And who are you?" Willy said.

"You remember Bill Swifburg, right?" Vince said as he pointed to the overweight kid with the sandy hair, "I'm sure you've seen him in the papers or around town. He played for the Tomahawks."

"What does he mean by 'Colt?'" Willy said.

"We are the descendants of the Pniese," Vince said. "For thousands of years, we have maintained order on Halloween, but every warrior can only serve until he's nineteen, then it must be passed down to a blood relative with few exceptions. The 'Colt' is the one that receives the training to take the Pniese's place."

"Why can't anyone over nineteen be a Pniese?" Willy said.

"Teen-agers perform this duty mainly because the supernaturals respect the young more than the old," Vince said. "Young people are very psychic and sensitive to the supernatural and in the teen-age years, they have the power and endurance to overcome most physical challenges."

"It's like comparing a mall security cop to an FBI agent," Cindy Daniels said. "They both have authority, but you're obviously going to take one more seriously than the other. That's the way the supernaturals feel about us compared to the rest of the Living."

"I think I understand," Willy said, then turned to Vince. "So you guys are the monster cops that I've always seen hanging around on Halloween night."

"Yes, we're the monster cops," Vince said. "We're also known as the Halloween warriors and what not. I guess those names sound more glamorous than 'Pniese.'"

"And this is your last year?" Willy said, "Now you want me to take your place? Is that it?"

Vince nodded.

"You guys are really freaking me out, aaaright?" Willy said, "I just wanted to go the movies, maybe get a CD afterwards, play a couple arcade games, and you guys throw this at me. Vince, I ain't never gettin' in a car with you again, man."

"I can't force you to accept," Vince said. "You have to do it on your own free will. You should know, however, that this position is a great honor. It's supposed to be passed down from relative to relative, but I don't have any young teens in my family. When Mike died, we got real tight and I consider you like a brother. The name of the Native American shaman you saw in your dream is Kama. He was the first Pniese and he gives final approval over the worthiness of the Colts. He deemed you worthy, do you remember?"

"Yeah, I remember," Willy said.

"If you take this position, your next six Halloween nights will be the most dangerous nights of your life. It's a lot of responsibility and there aren't a whole lot of rewards and I'm going to push you hard. Eventually, you'll have to train a successor as well. When I had my dream and got the caribou skin and came here, I was just as confused as you are right now."

"We all were," Jessey Sassacus said.

"We all had reasons not to do it," Vince said, "but something inside of us, some kind of instinct urged us to take this direction. What does your instinct tell you?"

Willy looked up at Vince then gazed into each Pniese's eyes. When he experienced déjà vu, he knew what his answer was.

"It says 'where do I sign?'"

CHAPTER
7

September 27

"Willy?" Shayla Hynes said as she nudged her son's shoulder, "Willy? Wake up."

"It's Saturday," Willy said as he pulled the covers over his head. "Let me go back to my coma, aaaright?"

"Vince is on the phone," Shayla said. "He says it's very important that he talks to you right now. Is everything all right?"

Willy pushed the covers far enough aside for him to look at his clock. It was six-thirty. His parents usually were up at this time, but on Saturdays, Willy demanded that he be allowed to sleep as long as he wished. He wasn't planning on getting up until noon.

"I'm gonna kill him," Willy said and took the portable phone from his mother's grasp. "What?"

"Hey," Vince's voice said over the phone, "isn't it a beautiful morning?"

"Oh yeah," Willy said. "Great day for sleeping. Tell me you got a real good excuse for calling me this early."

Shayla snickered, adjusted the belt on her bathrobe, and left the bedroom.

"Well, I'm sorry if I woke you up and what not," Vince said. "I thought you'd be watching *Boots* on TV."

"Aw, have a heart," Willy said. "It's too early for *Dora* jokes. What do you want?"

"You know where Jenilee's Gardens is?"

"Yeah."

"I need you to pick up a whole crop of wolfsbane," Vince said. "Ask for Jenilee and then deliver it to Bill Swifburg's house. You remember him?"

"What's a wolfsbane?" Willy said, "And how am I gonna get it to Bill Swifburg's house. I don't know how to drive and I have no clue where he lives."

"Figure it out. Remember, we're counting on you. Big responsibility, remember?"

Vince hung up before Willy could reply.

Willy threw the covers off his bed with a deep inhale and the putrid feeling of morning breath coating his mouth. He swung his bare legs to the side and scratched his lower back.

"Figure it out," he said, quoting Vince in his best moronic voice, "big responsibility, remember? We're counting on you." Returning to his normal speaking voice, "Lousy, sleep-robbing, dork."

CHAPTER 8

Willy felt like an idiot as he walked down Woodland Avenue. He pulled a rusty red wagon that he hadn't used in five years behind him. Not that he had a choice in the matter. At first, he thought that maybe he could get a ride from his parents, but then he would have to explain why and he wasn't about to go into detail on the events of the night before. Then he thought about biking it, but Vince said he had to pick up "a whole crop" of wolfsbane. The only problem was, he had no idea how much a crop was, let alone what wolfsbane was. It sounded like a show from *Animal Planet*. Then again, Jenilee's Gardens didn't sell animals. To top it all off, he had no idea whether or not this wolfsbane had to be paid for or if it was paid in advance. Either way, Willy was not about to fork over his allowance. His father gave him ten dollars a week for taking out the trash and raking the leaves and spending it on wolfpain or whatever it was called didn't sound the least bit appealing. Whatever exactly his task was, he hoped that the wrong crowd didn't see him with the wagon. Unfortunately, the wheel's squeaking was loud enough for most neighbors to notice.

The only good thing about this unclear situation was that the autumn sun gave off the right amount of comforting heat and when it got too warm for Willy's taste, a cool wind came to the rescue. He looked ahead to the Takahoshi's. Marty was sitting on his front porch as expected, singing and playing the guitar. It sounded like he was singing something from Neil Diamond or Bruce Springsteen, but every time he thought he heard a familiar note, the wagon's squeaking wheels drowned out the melody. As he walked closer, he recognized the song: "Kryptonite" by *3 Doors Down*.

Suddenly, Marty ceased on his song and listened to the annoying screeching that only came from wagon wheels. Willy was passing by. Marty laughed.

"Well, good morning, Willy. You sleep well?"

"How'd you know it was me?" Willy said.

"Cause I'm smart," Marty said. "And what's with the wagon?"

"How did—never mind," Willy said. "Vince calls me up at six-thirty and tells me that I gotta deliver something to Bill. You have any idea what a wolfsbane is?"

"Sure," Marty said.

"Well?"

"Well what?"

"Well what's wolfsbane?" Willy said, "I ain't playin' now, aaaright? It's too early for this. If you guys want me in your little Frankenstein club, I better get my questions answered."

"Wolfsbane is a plant," Marty said. He leaned his guitar against the ceramic pot that held the dying blue iris. "It has little flowers and is extremely poisonous."

"What does me fetching a plant have to do with—you know?"

"You'll find out soon enough."

"And it's only going to Bill?"

"Uh-huh."

"Why only Bill?"

"You'll find out soon enough."

"Do you realize how stupid I look carrying this wagon and how stupid I'm gonna look carrying this wagon once it's filled with pretty flowers?" Willy said.

"The important thing is not how you look, but how you feel," Marty said.

"I feel stupid."

"I would too if I were you," Marty said. "I mean pulling a wagon full of flowers around town? You could put on a dress and skip and you wouldn't look as bad."

"Why do I even bother?" Willy said. He began to walk down the yard. Over the wagon wheel's rusty whines, he heard Marty call his name. He stopped and about faced.

"Come here a second," Marty said.

Willy dropped the wagon's handle and approached the Takahoshi's front steps.

"It's all part of the initiation," Marty said. "I did the same chore myself when I was a Colt two years ago."

"I've heard that word a couple times now," said Willy. "Why do they call the replacement a Colt? It sounds like a piece of beef. Do I got to wear a bell around my neck or something?"

"I don't think so, although they might make you stick some wolfsbane flowers in your hair," Marty said.

"Say what?" Willy said.

"Kidding. The term 'Colt' means 'rookie' or 'beginner,'" Marty said. "You only have to go by that name on this particular Halloween night because it's your first time. All rookies have to go by that name. Next year, you'll get your own name."

"Oh? And what name do you go by?"

"I'm not going to say in public. Go do your errand. You'll find out soon enough."

CHAPTER 9

Willy pulled into the Jenilee's Gardens parking lot with tired legs and a screeching wagon that showed no mercy to his ears. Jenilee's Gardens was Sleepy Owl's only botany shop. The Indian summer thought long gone as early as yesterday, made an unexpected return. The sun had gone from welcoming to breathing fire on his back for the last half-hour. The sweat that dripped from his forehead had dampened his collar.

Being Saturday and the Halloween season, Jenilee's Gardens was crowded with cars. The side of the shop was busy with persons observing and scanning the variety of pumpkins. The painted jack o'lanterns were perched on shelves as they made funny and scary faces to the children that desired them. The bigger pumpkins were pig-piled in four large crates, where adults and bigger kids handled them. As Willy approached the entrance, he heard the townsfolk around him make their choices.

"Are you kiddin'? That's got a huge hole! It'll be rotten by Halloween!"

"Mommy, I want the pumpkin with the eyes that are crossed!"

"Hey, hey, hey! This here is a good one!"

"Do you like the one with the big stem or the little stubby one?"

"That one's too green."

"Honestly Ernest, you're worse than the kids."

The electric doors hummed and parted. Willy stepped into the spacious shop, relieved to be out of the sun. He was even more pleased that the wagon's grating wheels was barely heard because of the constant chatter. Jenilee's Gardens reeked of fertilizer as he walked further into the store. He made his way past a Halloween attraction made up of a bale of hay, several painted jack o'lanterns, and a cheerful-looking scarecrow. Below it was a sign that said, "Get your pumpkins early, Halloween is coming!"

Up ahead was a woman in a green apron. She was classifying flowers into thin green barrels that were filled with water. Her most distinguishing feature was the dark mole on her cheek and her overdone green eye shadow.

"Uh, excuse me?" Willy said. He noticed the "Jenilee's" logo on her apron and her nametag that said, "Barbara."

The woman turned to him and smiled as she snapped her gum. "Can I help you?"

"Uh, yeah," Willy said. "I need to get a whole bunch of wolfsbane. That's a real poisonous plant that's got these little flowers on 'em."

"Sorry, but we're all out of wolfsbane," Barbara said. "In fact, we've been all out of wolfsbane since July. We sell them in the spring."

"You sure about that?" Willy said. Agitation hammered his mind.

"Sure, I'm sure," Barbara said. "We have no wolfsbane whatsoever. Is there anything else I can help you with?"

"Yeah, you can point me to traffic. I feel like playing in it right about now."

"What's that, toots?" Barbara leaned closer.

"Uh, nothing," Willy said, "thank you very much."

Barbara smiled "good-bye" and went back to arrange her flowers.

Willy and his wagon rolled towards the exit, his insides ready to erupt. He was pulled out of bed on a Saturday to walk for over an hour to get a stupid weed or herb or whatever and now, they tell him that they've been sold out.

"Vince," Willy said, "you are so, so, so very dead."

CHAPTER 10

"**D**ude, where are the plants?" Bill Swifburg said.

Bill had answered his front door and saw Willy overheated, disgusted, and tired. Bill's house was three miles from Jenilee's Gardens. During that long journey, Willy heard a group of kids pick on him for carrying his kiddie wagon and was almost mangled by a Doberman whose chain leash was too long. Now, as he did the night before, Willy wanted answers.

"There are no plants. They've been sold out for a good five months. They get their shipments in the spring. Tell me you guys had a good reason for letting me walk with this stupid kid's wagon all over town only to pick up something that's sold out."

"You didn't ask for Jenilee, did you?" Bill said, "Don't you know that she owns the place?"

"Yeah, I know that," Willy said. "The name of the store kinda' tipped me off."

"Didn't Vince tell you to ask for her personally?" Bill said.

Willy went to respond with more sarcasm. His jaw was halfway open when he realized his slight error. He hadn't obeyed Vince's specific order. He groaned.

"Go to the driveway," Bill said. "I'll be out in a second."

The Swifburg's front door closed. Willy took hold of the wagon's handle and started down the walkway. As he headed towards the driveway, Willy noticed that Bill had a nice-looking home. The upper half was white with blue shudders and the lower half was made of brick. The garage was the biggest part of the house. It could hold up to six vehicles, even though Bill's parents, Richard and Priscilla Swifburg, were the only ones who had cars. Bill was saving for his own transportation and his younger sister, Jacqueline, was five years away from getting her driver's license. In the driveway was a dark green Ford Mustang, parked under a basketball net.

A loud grind was heard. Willy turned to his left. One of the automatic garage doors opened. Bill was behind it, dressed in a Sleepy Owl Tomahawks sweatshirt and jeans that were too tight to fit his 248-pound frame. He twirled a set of car keys with his finger and placed mirrored sunglasses over his green eyes.

"Put your wagon in the trunk and get in."

Richard Swifburg's car was fit. The carpet was vacuumed and the new car smell was still detected. Best of all, there was air conditioning: Willy's best friend today. Neither Bill nor Willy had said a word until they got to the end of Strong Elm Street. Bill pulled open the ashtray, which was clean and held a roll of *Certs*.

"Want any?" he said.

"No thanks," Willy said. "So what's the deal with the wolfsbane?"

"First, tell me how you knew where I lived," Bill glanced at Willy, then turned his attention back to the road.

Willy shrugged his shoulders. "It wasn't that hard. Vince told me your last name. All I had to do was go to Town Hall where my friend's mother works and use her computer. There it was: 101 Strong Elm Street."

"Good job, *Columbo*," Bill said. "I use wolfsbane as a weapon and for protection on Halloween night."

"Protection?" Willy said, "How can a plant protect you? What do you use it for? Poisoning?"

"No, nothing like that," said Bill. "It's used to ward off the undead and evil spirits. It stings like acid to them."

"No kidding." Willy raised his eyebrows, "But like I said, they're all out. It ain't gonna matter if you talk to the owner or not. How can you get wolfsbane if it ain't coming until next spring?"

"You'll find out soon enough," Bill said. He flicked on the right blinker.

Willy turned to his window and rolled his eyes. As his faint reflection stared back at him, he muttered, "I wish you guys would stop saying that."

CHAPTER 11

Willy was certain that there was no way they would find a parking space for at least ten minutes when they pulled into Jenilee's Gardens. To his surprise, however, Bill drove past the front lot and rolled up to the shop's left side where the trucks usually go to drop off shipments. Bill ignored the yellow "NO PARKING, DELIVERY AREA" sign and entered the back of Jenilee's Gardens. He put the green Ford Mustang in park.

"Yo, I don't think we can park here, man," Willy said.

"You'll –" Bill said.

"I know, I know. I'll find out soon enough."

As they approached the back door, a man noticed their intrusion, but smiled. He looked to be in his mid-fifties. He sported a brown beard that was crudely trimmed at the chin and was dressed in a checkered shirt and polyester pants.

"Bill Swifburg?" the man lowered his clipboard. "Is that you?"

"How are you doing, Mr. Crocker?" Bill said.

"I'm just fine," Mr. Crocker said. They shook hands. "I ain't seen you on the field this year. What's going on with that?"

"I got a little injury." Bill pointed to Willy, "This is Willy Hynes, a good friend of mine."

Mr. Crocker stuck out his hand. "Good to meet you, Willy."

"Yeah, what's going on?" Willy said. He shook Mr. Crocker's hand.

"Listen Bill," Mr. Crocker said. "I know you're a heck of a good player on the field, but this here is my job. I can't allow anyone to park back here, especially on busy days like today. It wouldn't be fair to the other customers. You understand me?"

"I don't wanna cause any trouble, Mr. Crocker," Bill said. "Could you tell Jenilee that I'm here?"

Mr. Crocker nodded. He went into the shop. After a few seconds, a slim, forty-year-old woman who looked ten years younger than that came out. She had blue eyes and blond hair that was mostly hidden under a red paisley headscarf. It was Jenilee.

"Hi, Bill," she said.

"Hi, Jenilee," Bill said and pointed his thumb at Willy. "Vince's Colt had a little problem finding you."

Willy's jaw fell open. He stared at Bill, then Jenilee.

"You're in on this too?" Willy said.

Simultaneously, Bill and Jenilee shot their index fingers to their lips with a loud "SSSSSHHHHHHHHHHH!"

"Yes," Jenilee said. "I mean I was. Over twenty years ago to be exact. I've heard a lot of good things about you from my daughter."

"Who's your daughter?" Willy said.

"Cindy," Jenilee said, "Cindy Daniels. She substituted at your school a little while ago, didn't she?"

"Yeah," Willy said. He gazed at Jenilee while concentrating on what Cindy Daniels looked like. He noticed that there was a resemblance in the shape and color of their eyes.

"You're here for the wolfsbane, right?" Jenilee said to Bill.

"Yeah," Bill said. "Should we follow you?"

"Uh-huh," Jenilee said. She and Bill began to walk away from the shop.

"Wait a second," Willy said. He jogged to catch up, "You had the dream? The one with the Indian chief and the animal skin and all that?"

"Yep," Jenilee said. "It was many years ago, but I had it all right. Didn't they explain all this to you at Huford House?"

"He's a slow learner," Bill said.

"Up yours," Willy said to Bill then turned to Jenilee. "Don't you get kinda worried that your daughter was hanging around a haunted house and what she does on Halloween? I know my folks would probably kill me if they found out."

Jenilee turned to Willy with the grin of a teacher to a student.

"You ask too many questions, kiddo," she said. "Just pay attention and let your instinct be your guide."

They walked past several bales of hay, stacked pyramid style, as well as a coiled-up garden hose and a broken pushcart before they came to a shack the size of an outhouse. The shack was padlocked, but hardly burglar proof. The wood was never treated and became rotten over the last few years. Jenilee's logo was recognized on the door, but the paint was chipped. She reached into her jean overall pocket and pulled out a ring that had more keys attached to it than a school custodian's did. She fiddled with them and finally found the right one. She snapped open the padlock.

"You're going to have to move quick," Jenilee said. "My employees think that we sold out of these a long time ago."

She took a fast look around, searching for Mr. Crocker or anyone else who shouldn't see the contents in the shack. The coast was clear. She pulled open the door. Inside were several ceramic pots, placed on the floor and shelf and wherever space was available in the cramped shack. Each red-clay pot had wolfsbane sprouting out of it. Most of them appeared healthy with their strong stems, spike-shaped leaves, and hooded flowers that were indigo like the sky before a thunderstorm. There were a few that were an ill yellow instead of green and the tips of some leaves were dried out, but Bill didn't seem to mind. The entire plant was used for his needs. He struggled to squeeze his hand into his ultra-tight jean pocket and managed to pull out his car keys. He gave them a quick twirl then handed them to Willy.

"The left button is for the trunk," he said. "Open it up and give me a hand. We're gonna empty this shed."

"Okay," Willy took the keys.

"I see the kid's got spunk," Jenilee said, as she watched Willy run back towards the Ford.

"I hope he'll be ready for Halloween," Bill said.

Jenilee chuckled. "No one ever is. Be sure to return my pots once you're through with them and be careful handling them this time."

CHAPTER 12

The door to the Hynes's house opened. Willy's afternoon was inconvenienced as he walked for miles to the garden store, then to Bill Swifburg's house, then helped unload the wolfsbane into Bill's basement. Bill never went into detail on how he will use the herb as a weapon against the creatures of the night and refused to give Willy a ride home.

"I gave you a break already by driving you back to Jenilee's," he said. "When someone's in training, they usually have to do it themselves."

So Willy walked all the way home again. His kiddie wagon rolled behind him. His thighs were sore and his shirt wet with perspiration. All he cared about now was going into the shower and calling his friend, Daryl, to hang out later in the evening. His mother, Shayla, was by the stove stirring a pot of tapioca pudding.

"Hey Willy," she said. "Where have you been all day?"

"Oh, here, there, and everywhere," Willy said. "Anyone call me?"

"Yeah, Daryl and Ian. What do you plan to do tonight?"

"Me? Just go hang with Daryl. Are you and Dad going out?"

"Yeah, it's Mikey Hendrik's birthday and the four of us are going to dinner," she said. "I'm making you this pudding in case you were going to stay home tonight."

"Can Daryl sleep over?"

"That's fine, just be in by nine-thirty. Don't make me worry about you."

"Yeah, okay," Willy said. "Well, I'm gonna take a shower."

Shayla turned the gas off. "Not yet. Your father is still in there and I've got to go next. You've got an hour's wait, I'd say."

Willy rolled his eyes and made a croak in his throat. He reached for the portable telephone and dialed. There was a pick-up after three rings.

"Hullo?"

"Yeah, it's me."

"Hey Willy, what's going on?" Daryl Julson said.

"Nothing really."

"Where have you been all day? My mother said you were walking down the street with your old wagon, cursing up a storm."

"Never mind. What're you up to doing tonight?"

"How about the arcades?"

"Sounds good, but I gotta be in by half past nine. You wanna sleep over?"

"Hold on a second," Daryl said and then screamed out. "MAAAAAAAAAAA?!"

There was a pause. Daryl took another breath.

"MMMMAAAAAAAAAAAAAAAAAAAAAA?!"

Another pause. Willy held the receiver away from his ear. Daryl was like being inside the XL Center during a sold out game. He could be exciting and deafening, but sometimes annoying.

"MMMMMMMAAAAAAAAAAAAAAAAAAAAAAAAAAAAAAAAAA?!"

"What is it, Daryl?!" his mother's faint, but booming voice said.

"CAN I SLEEP OVER WILLY'S?!"

"Fine!" she said.

"Hullo, Willy?" Daryl said, "My Mom said—"

"Yeah I know," Willy said. "As well as the rest of the neighborhood."

"Huh?"

"Nothing. Come over around six-thirty okay?"

"Okay, bye."

"Bye."

Willy hung up the phone and debated whether or not to call Ian. Ian was the kind of kid who was always at home. Whenever they got together, Ian had always suggested that Willy come to his house. Willy didn't mind under certain circumstances, but Ian's parents smoked as if they were having a race on who could get a voice box first. Their house stunk like cigars. Every time Willy left, his hair and clothes reeked and it took two showers or one long one to get the stench off his body. He was in no mood to put up with anything like that or its possibility and decided to call Ian tomorrow.

CHAPTER 13

Daryl came over at six-thirty as he said he would. His father waited in the car, ready to take them both to the *Arcade Palace* just outside of Sleepy Owl. Willy put on his *Oakland Raider*'s jacket and was ready to exit when his mother came down the stairs in a black cocktail dress and open-toed heels.

"Hold it," she said. "Do you have your key?"

"Yeah, Ma," Willy said. "I've also memorized the rules: no using the oven, no phone calls after ten, and no eating in the family room without a tray."

"Have fun tonight," Shayla said. "Give me a kiss."

"Maaaaa."

"Come on, it'll only take a second."

"Oh for God's sake," Willy muttered as he stepped over to his mother and kissed her cheek. He smelled her perfume and tasted a hint of her make-up.

Mr. Julson, Daryl's father, smiled at the boys as Willy got in the car and shut the door. Mr. Julson wore a faded *Celtics* baseball cap. The net-like structure on the cap's back half seemed to be tearing a little further apart with each time Willy saw him. Daryl was a lanky, red-haired kid, the same age as Willy. His freckles overwhelmed his face and his feet looked too big for the rest of his body.

"Now, I'm gonna take you guys to the video arcade place and pick you up at nine and bring you back here. Is that right?" He pulled out onto Woodland Avenue.

"That's right," Daryl said.

The car's inside was dark, but Mr. Julson's headlights and the streetlights above provided shape to where everything was. The radio station was also lit up with green numbers: 108.7. The disc jockey promised to play the best of the fifties and sixties.

"How's school so far this year, Willy?" Mr. Julson said.

"Just fine," Willy said. "Then again, it's only September and I'm sure things will get a lot tougher soon enough."

"Ah, I know what you mean," Mr. Julson said. "I had a terrible time in school. Have you thought about what you're going to be for Halloween?"

"It crossed my mind here and there," Willy said.

Daryl looked at him. "You're not actually gonna go trick-or-treating are ya?"

While Willy wasn't against the idea, before last night that is, Daryl believed that such an act was for kids only. If you were in junior high or above, you just went tricking.

"Probably not," Willy said. "It's still a long way off. I'll probably end up passing out candy or maybe do a little shaving cream action. Who knows?"

"I can't believe it," Mr. Julson said. He turned left and drove towards the town limits, "Halloween is the biggest franchise in this country except for Christmas. The whole town gets into it and you guys don't seem that interested."

"I personally don't see the point of it," Daryl said. "With other holidays, there are meanings behind them, but Halloween is just a time where you play dress-up and get candy. It's like a scary form of Valentine's Day."

"If you only knew…" Willy said.

"What?"

"Nothing."

CHAPTER
14

Willy and Daryl played all versions of *Mortal Kombat* as well as *Star Wars, Simpson's Bowling, House of the Dead, Pump It Up NX2*, and a bunch of pinball machines. By the time they were out of tokens, they still had more than an hour before Mr. Julson picked them up. They hung out in the parking lot near the entrance and got drinks from a vending machine: *Sprite* for Daryl, *Cherry Coke* for Willy.

"Anything good on TV tonight?" Daryl said.

"I don't know," Willy said. "If worse comes to worse, we'll just watch reruns or some DVD. Have you got any money left?"

Daryl reached into his pocket and pulled out a plastic wallet. He unfolded it and sifted his fingers through the slits. "I got a ten and three nickels. Why?"

"You wanna go next door and get a quick game of mini golf in?" Willy said.

Daryl hated to break his high bills. He came to the arcade with his ten dollar bill, along with seven ones and five quarters. When he was done with the small cash, he usually backed off. Boredom, however, was something Daryl hated even more than breaking a ten. If he was going to spend more money, he might as well have fun. It was a nice night anyway. "Yeah, I guess so."

The boys walked across the parking lot towards *Eighteen Holes and Eighteen Flavors*, the combination ice cream shop with a mini golf course on the side. The sky was black, which made the neon signs around them look even more luminous. Main Street was packed with zooming vehicles. Willy had guessed that the Sleepy Owl Tomahawks had beaten the Wilburton Rams tonight because some of the cars that passed by, the first being a convertible *Porsche*, were filled with screaming Tomahawks cheerleaders strangling their pom-poms in the air. The *Porsche*'s driver was still dressed in his football uniform. He half-stood up and said, "Number one, baby! Tomahawks rule! WWWOOOOOOOO!"

"Losers," Daryl said.

Willy could understand Daryl's comment. Because he wasn't athletic, Daryl dripped of jealousy, but at the same time, towns like Sleepy Owl gave football more attention than any other activity. If you weren't a Tomahawk or a Tomahawk supporter, you were a weirdo. Daryl was a weirdo because he disliked football. He played the clarinet and planned to join the high school band next year. Willy wasn't a weirdo because he watched the occasional game with Vince and used to see Bill Swifburg tackle rival players. He just wasn't obsessed with all the hoopla that went with it.

Willy attempted to change the subject. "So why did you use *Scorpion* this time? You always use *Raiden*."

Willy referred to *Mortal Kombat 4,* Daryl's favorite arcade game. Daryl's face lit up. "I've actually started to take a liking to him," he said. "I've re-discovered the game at home and I'm really starting to get his moves down."

"Yeah, I saw that 'Toasty Fatality' you did," said Willy as they crossed over to *Eighteen Holes and Eighteen Flavors.* "It was real sweet stuff."

When the boys got their golf balls and walked away from the cashier, they were met with a surprise. For Daryl, he was laying his eyes on Mary Anna Colinsworth, the girl that had stolen his heart. Mary Anna was taller than both Willy and Daryl by at least three inches and had red hair like Daryl, only much longer and silkier. She was lining up her putter and calculating how hard she should tap her yellow ball into the hole.

Willy was surprised because Jessey Sassacus, donned in her usual long flowered dress and moccasins, was with Mary Anna. Neither had seen the boys as they focused on their game. They laughed at Mary Anna's yellow ball as it half-circled the edge of the hole then traveled away. They were on the third hole, a family of three was on the second, and Willy had just put his blue ball down on the first.

Daryl stared at Mary Anna. "God, isn't she hot?"

"Oh yeah, she's all that," Willy said as he looked down at his ball. "You think I should ask her out?"

"Shut up," Willy said and swung his putter. The ball went through the windmill's door, narrowly missed the blades, and disappeared out the other side.

"What?"

"I said 'shut up.' I don't wanna go there tonight."

"What do you mean?" Daryl said. He put his red ball on the ground.

"I mean every time you see her, you say, 'God, isn't she hot? Should I ask her out? Do you think she likes me?' and you don't do nothin' about it. Every time you go to talk to her, you turn chicken and run away. So from now on, just don't bring her up, unless you plan to do something about it. Either take a crap or get off the toilet."

"I'm just taking it slow," Daryl said. His ball went through the windmill, "I'll make the move when the time is right."

"You been saying that for a year," Willy said. "How long do you need?"

Daryl thought for a moment. He watched Mary Anna approach the fourth hole and then turned to Willy. "You know what? You're right."

"I know I am," Willy said.

"Let's go."

"Say what?"

Daryl didn't answer his friend. He jogged over to the other side of the windmill and grabbed his ball. Willy followed and noticed that his ball was only an inch away from the hole.

"Daryl, where you going, man?"

"Grab your ball," Daryl said as he approached the family ahead of him. "It's time to take my crap!"

"Aw man, why now?"

"Excuse me, sir?" Daryl said to the father of the family. "Would you mind if we went ahead of you? We're in a little bit of a hurry."

"Not at all," the father said.

"Thank you," Daryl said. "Come on, Willy."

Daryl zigzagged past the third hole and came upon the fourth. Jessey Sassacus was ready to aim her green ball up a long hill. Mary Anna sat on the bench across from Jessey and was tying her tennis shoes.

"Hi, Mary Anna," Daryl said, slightly out of breath.

"Oh, hi Daryl," Mary Anna said.

Jessey's ball climbed the hill.

"Your turn," she said to Mary Anna and noticed Willy behind Daryl. A smirk drew across her face as she backed away from the tee area.

"So, how's things?" Daryl said to Mary Anna.

"Good," she said and placed her yellow ball down.

Jessey approached Willy. She used her putter as a cane.

"Your friend's got a little crush on my friend, huh?" she half-whispered.

"You don't know the half of it," Willy whispered back.

"I heard you were walking around town today with a kid's wagon," Jessey said. "They say you were uttering some real interesting vocabulary."

"I really hate small towns, you know that?" Willy said. As he bounced his ball on the pavement trail that guided golfers to their next obstacle, Willy noticed Jessey's arms. Long and pale scars made their mark across her forearms. The thickness of them had tightened Willy's heart. His imagination listed scenarios on how she could have received such fatal slashes.

Jessey snickered. "I did the same kind of things last year. It's for a good cause, you know that."

"No, I don't know that," Willy said, leaning towards her ear. "All I know is that I pulled an animal skin out'a my dream and now I belong to some secret club that has me running around town to get plants cause we need them against the undead."

"You'll understand more as we get closer to Halloween," Jessey said. "Believe me, I know wh—"

"What are you guys talking about?" Mary Anna said.

"Nothing," Willy and Jessey said together.

CHAPTER 15

"She was all over me tonight," Daryl was lying on top of Willy's bed, gazing at the ceiling.

"Oh yeah," Willy said, "she couldn't take her eyes off ya."

Daryl flipped to his stomach and leaned toward Willy who was going through his CD collection. "You really think so?"

"I don't know," Willy said. "The girl smiled a lot. That could mean that she's either humoring you or she likes you. Personally, if someone were hovering over me like a vulture, I'd be a little turned off. You seen my *L.L. Cool J* CD?"

"No," Daryl said. "So you think I blew it?"

Willy groaned. "Daryl, I don't wanna get into it anymore. Can't we talk about something other than your war with puberty?"

Daryl rolled onto his back again and resumed his ceiling gaze. His hands found their way to the back of his head. Willy continued to scour through his CDs, trying to find one that he wasn't sick of hearing. It was after midnight and his parents forbid the use of the television, but Willy and Daryl were allowed to do anything within reason in Willy's room as long as they were quiet. Willy pulled out *AC/DC* and fed it into his CD player. He put the volume on #3 and pushed "play."

"Her friend is an oddball, huh?" Daryl said.

"Who?" Willy said, "Jessey?"

"Yeah. Remember she went to school with us last year? She's always wearing moccasins and those Indian earrings and she's always reading about Indian stuff."

"So she's into her heritage. So what?"

"That's all she's into though. I ain't seen her at any parties, she hardly says a word to anyone other than Mary Anna. I don't know about you, but I don't trust no girl who's that secretive. Did you see that gash on her arm?"

"Yeah."

"I heard a rumor that she tried to commit suicide last Halloween."

"I didn't know you kept tabs on her life," Willy said as he got up and approached a nearby shelf. He picked up a *Nerf* football that rested on the middle shelf, among a handful of trophies from his years in the Pee Wee leagues.

Daryl spun onto his stomach again. "I don't. I just noticed these things. A lot of guys do. You know her folks are rich. Her father owns one of those big fancy casinos in Hartford."

"So I'm told," Willy said. He tossed the football in the air and caught it on the way down.

"Maybe she thinks she's better than everyone else," Daryl said. "You know, maybe she's like a rich snob and that's why she doesn't talk to a lot of people."

"I don't think that's it at all," Willy said. "She talked to me, didn't she? Maybe she's just real grown up for her age. Either way, I don't care."

"What exactly did she say to you tonight?" Daryl said as he dug his elbows into the mattress and rested his chin in his palms.

"She was wondering why I hung out with someone as poor as you."

"What? Really?"

"No," Willy said. "Now get off my bed."

CHAPTER 16

September 28

"Why won't you let me sleep?" Willy said into the phone receiver. Like the day before, Shayla Hynes had crept into Willy's bedroom, nudged him, and told him that Vince Thomason was on the phone.

"Look out your window," Vince said.

Willy turned 180 degrees and looked out the window with his sleep, dust-covered eyes. It was five forty-five in the morning and the sun was almost done pulling itself to the top of the purple and blue-shaded sky. Vince Thomason stood in the middle of the street in gray sweatpants and a *Notre Dame* sweatshirt. He had one ear against his cell phone as he waved at his protégé.

"It's jogging time," he said.

"Great," Willy yawned, "have fun."

"No, you don't get it," Vince said. "You're coming with me. I want you down here in five minutes."

"I got company over."

"Who?"

"Daryl. He slept over last night."

"You'll be back before he even wakes up. Come on, up and adam."

"I don't wanna," Willy said, giving himself a look of disgust as he caught a whiff of his morning breath.

"I know," said Vince. "Five minutes."

Willy came out the front door in his father's sweatshirt and still in his flannel pajama bottoms. Vince stuffed his cellular into his pocket.

"Morning, sunshine," Vince said as traces of his breath were seen in the chilly atmosphere. If Willy had the strength, he would have given the finger.

They jogged side by side up Woodland Avenue. Thin steam escaped their mouths and primordial sunlight stung their eyes. Vince appreciated the tranquility that came with an early morning jog. There was no one out except the paperboys, the occasional other jogger, and small brown rabbits that munched on the grass in front yards. Willy, on the other hand, concentrated on getting the jog over with so he could go back to his bed that was too warm for him to have left in the first place.

"I need you to do another errand today," Vince said.

"What?" Willy said.

"I need you to go to *Don's Jewelry* and pick up a package and then bring it to Cindy. Remember her?"

Willy managed to nod while he released a long yawn.

"What kind of package?" he said.

"Just a regular package, no big deal," Vince said. "Oh, and don't make any plans tonight cause we gotta go to the *Walnut Inn*."

"What's at the *Walnut Inn*?"

"A pool."

"We're going swimming?" Willy said as they reached the end of Woodland Avenue and turned left onto Jenkins Avenue.

"Sure are," Vince said. "Every Sunday until November. I want you to be ready by six o' clock."

"I've got homework you know," Willy said.

"You'll be back by seven-thirty, eight at the latest. I'll give you a hand with your math if you need it."

"That's okay," Willy said. His breathing grew heavy. "Vince, I've been thinking."

"What about?"

"Tell me again what it is we're going to be dealing with on Halloween."

"Just about every creature that this world says is a fake," Vince said. "I know that's a little hard to believe and what not, but it's true."

"Like what?" Willy said, "You mean vampires, werewolves, zombies?"

"Yes on vampires and zombies. Not to mention ghosts, goblins, witches, elves, and a whole bunch more that I can't think of," Vince said. "Werewolves only show up if Halloween falls on a full moon."

"You're right, it is hard to believe," Willy said. "It's not that I don't believe you completely, it's just hard to swallow. I mean, who in his right mind would believe that things like that exist?"

"Look at it this way: every legend is based on some truth. Where do you think people came up with the ideas for these creatures?"

"Okay, so on Halloween night, where do they come from?"

"That's easy. The Netherworld."

"No, I mean how do they get here?" Willy said, "Do they come through a magic door or people's closets or a *Greyhound* bus, what?"

"No, nothing like that," Vince said. "Some of them rise out of the lakes or come out from deep in the forests. Some even fall from the sky, believe it or not. No one actually sees it happening, but they've told me that's how they get here. You see, they can only pass into this world through a natural element, like water, earth, air, and sometimes, fire. The undead sometimes come out of tombs. It really depends on what species we're talking about."

"So how long are they allowed to stay here?" Willy said

"Four hours, six o'clock to ten," Vince said. "That's the curfew."

"And just what happens if they don't go back to their world?"

"You ever heard of the Abominable Snowman or the Loch Ness Monster or the Winsted Wildman?"

"Yeah."

"That's what happens," Vince said. "The actual curfew is midnight. We just end it at ten because often times, we need those extra two hours to round up the wanderers and trouble-makers. Sometimes though, we can't get to all of them and they're forced to stay here on the Earth for the next year. During that time, they're on their own and if they come in contact with people, chaos often follows. Just look at how many people have flocked to the northwest in order to catch a glimpse of Bigfoot."

"You mean to tell me there are Monster Cops in these places too?"

"The 'Monster Cops,' as you say, are all over the world. Here, we're called the Pniese. In Canada and Tibet and Australia and what not, they go by a different name, but they all have the same goal: to protect people and supernaturals from each other."

They strode onto Enfield Street and arrived minutes later on Baykok Avenue, home of the infamous Huford House. Although Vince reassured Willy that the spirits inside the edifice wouldn't harm him, Willy still couldn't help but feel nervous as he trotted closer. It was kind of like getting a shot at the doctor's office. When it's done, you wonder what the big deal was, but the next time you see a needle, those old fears always resurface no matter how much you've grown up. When they reached 112 Baykok Avenue, Vince stopped jogging and looked at his watch.

"Thirty-three minutes."

"Pretty good." Willy said as he subsided in front of Huford House and pointed, "We're not going in there today, are we?"

"No, today we train," Vince said. "The warm-up is over. You ready for the challenge?"

Willy fell into astonishment as he tried to catch his breath. The side of his rib cage ached from the jog. Though it wasn't his style to show vulnerability, he palmed his hip anyway. "That was the warm-up?"

"Oh yeah," Vince said. "We jogged. Now, we're gonna run back to your house and we're gonna time it. You need to build speed and endurance and what not. Believe me, the last thing you want is to be out of shape on Halloween."

"One more question before we start."

"Go ahead."

"Will *King Kong* and *Godzilla* show up on Halloween?"

"No, don't be ridiculous," Vince said. "Only real monsters show up."

"Oh," Willy said, "silly me."

Vince leaned his upper body forward while his legs bent and twitched as they revved themselves up for a sprint. "You ready?"

Willy took a deep breath and turned his head to spit. He positioned himself as Vince did. "Ready."

"GO!"

Willy darted up Baykok Avenue as fast as he could. Though Vince could go faster, he ran juxtapose with his friend. Together, they ran towards the end of Baykok Avenue, onto Enfield Street, Jenkins Avenue, Woodland Avenue, and eventually, came to the Hynes home. Throughout their run, Vince made frequent glances at his watch and frowned. True, Willy just started in his training and he was faster than the average thirteen-year-old boy was, but Vince still couldn't help but wonder if it was right that Willy was involved in this. After all, the Pniese was primarily for family bloodline and keeping this secret from Willy's parents was going to make it even more difficult. What's worse is if something awful happened to Willy, how would he ever explain it to Marvin and Shayla Hynes? Pniese have been hurt in the past. Pniese have also died and not all that long ago.

For Willy, the feeling of déjà vu returned when Vince yelled, "GO!" He wasn't into New Age things, but he was positive that he had somehow done all this before.

It took twenty-six minutes for Willy to return home from Huford House.

"Not bad," Vince said, as he looked at his watch. "Not good either."

Vince told him that he needed to get up every morning and run until he could do two miles in half that time. He also reminded Willy three more times to take care of the errand he was assigned to. Willy had offered Vince breakfast. Marvin Hynes fixed chocolate-chip pancakes every Sunday for his family and anyone who visited. Vince declined and told Willy to start eating a better balanced diet of vegetables and meat.

"It's only one month a year," he said. "Try to tough it out and I'll see you later on tonight around six."

"Aaaright," Willy said and wished more than ever that he could have those pancakes.

The feeling of fatigue returned like a boomerang by nine o'clock. Willy ate two fried eggs and a glass of orange juice then announced to his parents that he was going back to bed. Up the stairs he went, taking off his father's sweatshirt along the way, exposing his dark bare chest. When he reached his room, he stepped over his sleeping friend and plopped onto his bed. He pulled the flannel covers over him and nuzzled into dreamland within five minutes.

Less than ten minutes later, Daryl shook him. "Let's go get some breakfast."

Willy groaned. He pressed his face into his bed and donned his pillow like a hat as it covered the back of his head. "Why me?"

CHAPTER
17

"The jewelry store?" Daryl said as he peddled his bike, "Why do you want to go there? I thought we were going to catch a matinee?"

"I have to do an errand for Vince first," Willy said. They stopped at the corner of Jenkins Avenue and Main Street. Being a Sunday, there were a fair number of cars out. Willy saw *Gold's Supermarket* in the distance. Its parking lot was packed. Despite being closed for the last three weeks, *Duvall's Ice Cream* parking lot was three-quarters full as well. Daryl looked left and right and waited for the appropriate moment to come when he and Willy could petal to the other side of Main Street.

"Now let me get this straight," Daryl said. "We gotta get a piece of jewelry and then go all the way to the other side of town and give it to Vince? What does he think we are? His servants or something?"

"No, I gotta give it to a friend of his," Willy said. "She doesn't live that far."

"She?" Daryl said, "Who's 'she?' His girlfriend or something?"

"No," Willy said. Daryl's questions and the traffic on Main Street were an irritating combination. Finally, there was a gap between the passing cars. Willy looked to his right and saw no vehicles coming.

"Now!"

The two boys peddled across Main Street to the opposite side and then headed towards *Don's Jewelers*, which was a half-mile away.

"Why did you agree to do this?" Daryl said, "Doesn't Vince have a car? Why can't he do it himself?"

"He's probably busy," Willy said as they passed *Wendy's*.

"Busy with what? Mechanics don't work on Sundays. I hope this is nothing illegal cause I can be considered an accessory and—"

"Daryl," Willy said, "just shut your trap."
And he did.

Don's Jewelry was small and family-owned like most businesses in
Sleepy Owl. The owner, however, was far from an average jeweler. The
title under Don Desmond's business cards stated that he was a "master
craftsman." He could create just about anything a person could want. If
someone wanted a feather made of solid gold, all Don needed to do was
make a mold from a feather, then melt the gold and pour it in the mold.
There were other complications of course, but that was the basic idea.
When Willy reached the store and chained up his bike, he remembered
that his father had done business with Don Desmond. Marvin Hynes
bought a specially designed stickpin for Shayla on their anniversary.
Willy's father was impressed and talked about how Don Desmond was
in great demand all over Connecticut and even out of the state for his
creativity.

Willy and Daryl stepped inside. They felt the air conditioner, which
left Willy to regret not wearing his *Oakland Raiders* jacket. The store
was made mostly from glass. Display cases, lined with black velvet,
occupied most of the room. To Willy and Daryl's left were diamond
rings and earrings. To their right were gold and silver necklaces and
watches. Up ahead were rubies, emeralds, and platinum. Don Desmond
was behind the display as he got up and smiled at the boys. He was a
short old man with tanned skin and white balding hair.

"Hey, fellas."

"Hey," Willy said as he and Daryl stepped closer.

"I don't see a lot of boys your age coming in here," Don said. "What
can I do for you?"

"I'm here to pick up a package of some kind," Willy said. "Vince
Thomason said you have one for me."

Don's smiled faded. He looked curiously at Daryl, then turned his
attention back to Willy and nodded.

"Oh. Yeah," he said. "Sure, I'll go get it. Hold on."

He walked to the back of the store and opened the last door on his
right. His feet were heard as they hammered to the second floor. After
a few minutes, the hammering returned and the door opened again. Don
held a box made of black velvet that was the size of a clock radio. He

approached the back of the main display case and extended the box to Willy.

He gave Willy a quick wink. "Here you go. Is that all?"

"Yeah," Willy said. "At least I think so."

"Okay then," Don sat down in his chair and picked up his copy of the *Sleepy Owl Sunday Times*, "have a nice day."

Daryl's curiosity overwhelmed him when they left the store. He reached for the black velvet box. "Let's check it out."

"No," Willy kept the box as far from Daryl as he could.

"Why not? We're doing this stupid errand. We've earned the right."

"No," Willy got on his bike.

"Aw, come on. Aren't you even a little interested?"

"No." But that was lie.

CHAPTER
18

Cindy Daniels bit her middle fingernail and paced her room with the cordless phone kissing her ear. While Chris Tollen, her current boyfriend, talked of future plans, she glanced over at her Child Psychology book and wondered how she was going to pull off the mid-term scheduled a week before the annual sacred duty. Chris Tollen usually spoke with a deep and charismatic voice, but when he complained, it bordered on pitiful.

"I'm busy tomorrow night," she said into the receiver. "No, I'm not blowing you off…Chris…Chris…this next month is just a real busy time for me, that's all…I got exams, that's what…Look, it's not just classes. I have to spend time with these kids as part of my grade, then I got work, there's my Dad's birthday, b-b-bah…No, I haven't met anyone new. Jeez! Why are you trying to drive me up the wall?…Chris…Chris, I don't wanna fight…I don't wanna fight…that's got nothing to do with it…No, I don't regret that. In November, things are gonna be a whole lot easier…"

The doorbell hummed.

Cindy trotted out of her bedroom and made her way down the steps. A faint buzz of static clouded Chris's statements. Cindy debated about whether to ask him to repeat what he said or if she was better off not knowing.

"I've got someone at the door, hold on," she said.

She opened the front door. Willy Hynes and Daryl Julson stood behind the glass storm door. Cindy gave Daryl the same quizzical look that Don the jeweler had earlier. She held up a finger and turned her attention back to the cordless phone.

"I've got to go," she said. "Yeah, it's a guy…no check that, it's two guys…They're thirteen, Chris. Thanks for the trust…Yes…yes, I'll call you later on tonight…I promise…I will…I'm not going to forget…b-bye…yes…yes…okay…all right…bye."

The phone "beeped" as she pushed the "on/off" button with her thumb.

"Aye-yai-yai," she said.

She pushed the storm door open. The boys were invited in. Willy and Daryl noticed that incense slithered in the air as they looked around. The Daniels' home was chipper, from the bright pink carpet on the floor to the spot-free mirror on the same wall as the front door. Over to the left, Willy noticed that their closet door was open. Inside, among the shoes and sneakers was a pair of white *Roller Blades*. This struck a strange nerve with Willy. The size of the skates seemed to match Cindy's feet, but she didn't seem like the kind that roller-bladed. Usually, the roller-bladers that Willy saw were at *Derby Town*, a place outside of Sleepy Owl that had bowling alleys, a pizza restaurant, and a roller derby under one roof. It wasn't a typical hangout for college students. Before his thoughts could wander off any further, Cindy sat near the bottom of the stairs and asked what was up.

"Nothing really," Willy said. He handed her the black velvet package, "I was told to give you this."

Cindy accepted the box. "Did this come from the jewelry store?"

"Yeah," Daryl said, "be sure to tell Vince not to ask us to do any more favors for him until we get our licenses."

"You guys did this together?" Cindy stared at Willy.

"Yeah," Willy shrugged his shoulders. "Is everything okay?"

"Yeah," Cindy said and got up from the stairs. "Thanks a lot, guys. I got some things to do, so you'll have to excuse me."

She saw Willy and Daryl to the door. Once they were gone, she went into the kitchen. The phone receiver reunited with the cradle as she made her way towards the flowered dinner table. She sat down and pushed the wax fruit centerpiece aside. She opened the black velvet package. Rows of broad arrowheads were exposed. There were between twenty and thirty of them. It always depended on how busy Don was. One thing was a certainty. The arrowheads were always made from silver.

CHAPTER 19

V ince looked displeased when Willy got into the blue Mercury Sable. Willy waited for Vince to say what was on his mind as the vehicle shifted out of park and pulled out of the driveway. Vince said nothing at first. He made a loud sigh, letting the steam out of his big nostrils.

The sun had refashioned its look from afternoon white to a deep orange. Looking like a healthy pumpkin, it began its slow journey to the bottom of the sky, behind the dark and balding oak trees. Its rays were still warm as they penetrated through the windshield and poked Willy's vision. Willy folded down the car's sun visor, but it barely helped since he was only five feet, two inches. Vince stared ahead at the street like a first-time driver and gave another sigh through his nose. Willy could take it no longer.

"Spit it out, Vince," he said, "whatever it is."

"I got a call from Cindy a little while ago," Vince said. "She told me that you did the errand I assigned to you."

"Yeah," said Willy, "go on."

"She said that Daryl was with you the whole time. Is this true?"

"Yeah. So?"

"So this is supposed to be a secret." Vince glanced at him, "Daryl has nothing to do with the Pniese. We can't let certain people get suspicious of what we're doing."

"It's not a big deal," Willy said. "He had no idea what we were picking up or delivering. Come to think of it, I don't even know what it was either."

"That's not the point," Vince said. He turned off of Woodland Avenue, "The point is when we get ready for Halloween, you don't get others involved. Unless they're former or current Pniese members or close allies, you leave everyone out of it. That means *everyone*. Do you realize what would happen if the people in this town found out that half the creatures seen on Halloween night were real? There would be total anarchy. It's our job to make sure they don't know."

"Oh for God's sake," Willy said, "what do you want me to do about it?"

"From now on," Vince said, "Daryl, and no one else for that matter, goes with you to do anything that involves the Pniese."

CHAPTER 20

Willy gasped for air as his head skyrocketed out of the lukewarm water.

"Thirty seconds." Vince looked at his waterproof watch.

"Well?"

"Not bad. Not good either."

"That's right, build my confidence," Willy said.

"You got to hold it for at least ninety seconds," Vince said.

Willy rolled his eyes. He swam to the shallow end, passing under the thick blue beaded rope, until he could stand up without being underwater. The *Walnut Inn*'s pool was spacious and empty on Sunday nights. A red sign with large white letters saying, "SWIM AT YOUR OWN RISK!" rested on the chair reserved for the lifeguard. The area stunk of an overdose in chlorine. Willy's vision was cloudy.

"Are we really gonna have to go swimming on Halloween?" he said.

"Maybe," Vince said. "You have to be ready for anything."

"Whoa."

"What?"

"I just got another déjà vu," Willy said. "That's been happening a lot lately."

"All the Colts go through it. It's perfectly natural," Vince said. "You ready?"

Willy took three deep breaths and nodded.

"Go!" Vince said as he pointed at his student and looked to his watch.

Willy plunged under the water again. A series of bubbles rose to the surface and belched. A small splash occurred as Willy's feet kicked the surface. Vince's eyes shifted from Willy to his watch and back again.

It was crucial for all Pniese members to be able to hold their breath for at least a minute and a half, not only for underwater investigations, but on land as well. Evil spirits and hairy humanoids have been known to give off horrendous odors. These foul stenches are usually harmless, but Vince had heard of cases where they were deadly. One particular case Vince heard of came from his grandfather. It seemed that a friend of his was a Pniese member out in Illinois and during the fall of 1944, an entity called the Mad Gasser had caused a reign of terror in a small town called Mattoon. Vince had never seen or heard of such an entity in the Sleepy Owl area, but his grandfather had told him that the Mad Gasser was another example of why the supernaturals must leave before midnight.

Willy broke through the water and panted.

"Thirty-two seconds," Vince said. "Not bad. Not good either."

CHAPTER 21

SOUTHERN LOUISIANA
October 2

The evening was going so well too. Dana and her boyfriend, Chuck, saw the Broadway musical, *The Phantom of the Opera* and topped it off with a fabulous dinner at *Mona Maison's*, the finest restaurant in the area where the napkins are made of cloth and the crayfish cost over ten dollars. Chuck had even closed in for a major smooch when they got to the parking lot. The perfect date was coming to a close.

Chuck saved for a month to afford the theatre tickets and the expensive dinner, but there wasn't enough money to tune up his car. When it broke down on the side of the road an hour ago, both of them wondered if they would have been better off seeing the *Phantom* and then going to *Arby's*, which was closer to where they lived. It was eleven o'clock. Their cell phones had no reception. If a gas station was open, it wouldn't offer its welcoming lights for at least another two miles. Chuck hadn't spoken since he left his car and understandably so. Walking up a deserted road in the middle of the night caused his heart to grow heavy with fear. Dana's outlook was more positive. True, she found the road to be scary because there were no streetlights and nothing but woods on both sides. The trees themselves looked like they were closing in on them, but Dana found it exhilarating. The rush she felt almost made her forget the aching in her feet from walking in high-heels.

She hooked her arm around Chuck's and said in her Cajun accent, "Come on, it be all right."

"I know," Chuck said in a Cajun accent of his own. "I jus' feel better when we get to a station and let my folks know dat everything okay. Dey be worried by now."

"Creepy road, ain't it?" Dana said, "It's exciting, no?"

"Excitement I can do without, Cher," Chuck said. "I don't understand why dey don't put no night lights out here."

"It not so bad," said Dana. "The theatre was darker dan dis. Someday, we look back and dis and laugh, yes?"

"Yes, I guess so," Chuck said. He pulled her closer, "But I still want to get to a gas station as soon as possible."

Their feet's light rapping and the melody of nearby crickets were all that was heard as they made their way up the road, heading for more darkness, and hoping that a gas station or at least a sign would come across their sights. Chuck felt the side of Dana's head lean on his shoulder and deep down, wished he could do the same. But he was the man and men need to be strong in these spooky situations.

"What dat?" Dana sprung up from Chuck's shoulder.

There were mixed feelings when they saw the red light flicker on the left side of the road. It was the brightest light they had seen in the last hour, but what it was, they couldn't guess. The forest's dead leaves stirred as the blazed crimson blinked and nodded closer. It took the shape of a softball-sized orb. Dana wandered away from Chuck's embrace and started to cross the road. Her eyes were fixed on the light.

"Dana, where you going?"

Dana didn't answer. She made her way across the bank and approached the edge of the forest. For a second, she was ready to use common sense and turn back. Feelings of dread crawled up within her and pleaded for a physical retreat, but it was the light. She couldn't turn away from it. It held her interest like junk food would to someone on a diet.

Chuck placed his hand on her shoulder.

"Dana, get away from—"

Chuck's eyes caught the blazing orb. It shined with an illumination that rivaled floodlights during football night games and an evil beyond anything that nature could create. Though their minds screamed for help, Chuck and Dana's eyes fell blank and dilated. No matter how hard they tried to retreat, it was no use. All they could do was observe the red orb and the wicked shadow behind it.

"Voodoo rum," a graveled voice said from the darkness. "Jack needs his voodoo rum."

Chuck and Dana saw that the glow was coming from inside a metal lantern, held by a scorched hand. The lantern's owner stepped closer to them. The red glow showed its hideous face. Its skin was a sickening olive green. Its huge eyes were orange. It looked like a man, but there was something deformed and monstrous about it that couldn't possibly pass for a human. Its nose was turned up and wrinkles dominated the face. When the thing known as "Jack" smiled, Dana and Chuck wanted to cry for help, but they didn't. Their speech was just as crippled as their bodies. Jack had the kind of smile that came from a hunter after snagging its prey.

"Jack needs his voodoo rum," it said as its hand reached for Chuck. Jack didn't claw or strangle or maim. His free hand felt along Chuck's arms, ribcage, and hips. A sneer of disappointment shifted on Jack's face as he turned to Dana and gave her the same search. There was no voodoo rum for him tonight and that was enough to spark his temper.

"Go!" He pointed to the forest.

Chuck and Dana walked. They didn't want to. They wanted to run away faster than any squirrel, but they walked—going deeper into the woods. They tried to turn back and head for the street. On the street, there stood the chance of being seen and rescued, maybe even getting a logical explanation of who Jack was and how he was able to control them with his lantern. Their bodies just wouldn't cooperate. They were going to vanish into the forest and become one with its shadows whether they liked it or not. Chuck and Dana were gripped with cold fright as their feet trampled on swamp water. It was warm, but that didn't ease their panic as algae clung to their clothes and the water climbed up to their chests. They will drown. Unless, of course, the alligators got to them first.

Jack pushed his wavy hair to the side and donned his musty top hat. He held up his lantern and noticed that the red glow was flickering… dying. After all these years, the cursed piece of coal was being used up. The end of the long walk will soon be over. He will be free. Nothing will stop him then. It was only a matter of time. For now though, he must walk as he was condemned to many years ago. He is only allowed to stop for a few seconds. Perhaps when there was a chance to drink voodoo rum. Somehow, his always tired and sore feet managed to go on because they had to. By next week, he would probably be in South Carolina. The week after that, the best guess is Pennsylvania. By the end of the month, Jack will be in New England, perhaps Connecticut.

CHAPTER 22

October 15

Willy had become used to Huford House by now. Over the past two weeks, he had jogged every morning, ate salads more often, and went to the *Walnut Inn* pool every three days. His old jogging record of twenty-six minutes was now twenty-one minutes. He can now hold his breath underwater for fifty-five seconds. Yet, no matter how much he improved, Vince uttered the same comment over again: "Not bad, not good either."

Willy threw a punch at Jessey Sassacus.

She blocked it and using his momentum, sent him to the ground, his body dragging across the mats. Willy had worn boxing gloves, but they seemed unnecessary now. For the past thirty minutes, he hadn't been able to land a blow on the girl Daryl Julson called an "oddball."

"Did you see how I used your weight and power against you?" Jessey said.

Willy turned over onto his back and stared at the basement ceiling. It was an orange-brown color that blinked black because of the lit candles around them. Electricity would have been more convenient, but "abandoned" houses don't require such luxuries.

"Yeah, I see how," Willy said and rose off his back. "I've seen for the last half-hour. When do you get to take the bumps?"

"When you get focused," Jessey extended her hand.

Willy took it and ascended back to his feet. "I'm focused."

Before he could blink, his buttocks were back on the mat. Jessey had flipped him. "No, you're not," she said.

"It's a good thing this is all happening down here. You realize how humiliating it would be if someone saw me getting smacked around by…"

Jessey's brown eyes pierced through Willy's. Though her features were neutral, there was a slight offensiveness in her gaze. She folded her arms and waited for him to finish.

"Uh," Willy said, "never mind."

Jessey planted herself across Willy. She crossed her legs Indian style and pulled her hands out of her own padded gloves. "What's wrong?"

"What do you mean?" Willy said.

"I mean you're not focused on the matter at hand because your brain is playing the same show over and over again and somehow, it's still grabbing your interest."

Willy took off his boxing gloves and placed them between his sneakers and Jessey's bare feet. He let out a deep breath. "It's Vince."

"What about him?"

"He's getting to be a pain. No matter what I'm doing, it's just not good enough for him. I mean, hey, *he* chose *me* to succeed *him* in this whole Monster Cops thing and then he doesn't even put any faith in me."

"Vince is a tough cookie, it's true," Jessey said. "But he's a whole lot tougher on himself than he could ever be on you. He loves you a lot, you know."

"Oh God, don't tell me that." Willy rolled his eyes.

"He does, I can tell. Vince just wants you to be as ready as possible."

"But I need to know that he'll trust me when the time comes."

"I understand," said Jessey. "Do you want me to talk to him?"

"Naw, it's my problem," Willy said.

"You're part of a team now." Jessey smiled, "Your problems are our problems."

"It's aaaright."

"Are you sure?"

"Yeah, I'll take care of it."

"Okay. I want you to close your eyes," Jessey said.

"Why?"

"Because you're the Colt and I told you to. Now shoosh and close your eyes."

Willy did.

"I want you to breathe in deeply through your nose and then out through your mouth. Whatever troubles or anxieties that are going on through your mind, I want you to shut them out, just concentrate on your breathing."

Willy obeyed. His tense shoulders began to wind down. Willy felt his mind clear as tranquility crept up within him. If Jessey hadn't continued speaking, he believed that he could have dozed off and collapsed on the floor.

"Nothing else matters but your breathing," Jessey said in a soft voice. "I'm going to count back from five. When I'm done, you'll slowly open your eyes. Five...four...three...two...one."

His dark eyes opened to an orange blur, then focused to see the basement become familiar again. Jessey kneeled in front of him and held his hands in hers. "Do you feel better?"

"Yeah, actually I do," Willy said. "That's pretty good stuff."

"Meditation is a very healthy way to release aggression," Jessey said. "I use it quite a bit. Are you focused now?"

"Yeah, I think so," Willy said.

"Good," Jessey said. She released her grip from his hands. "Now let's see what you're made of."

As Jessey got up, Willy couldn't help but notice the candlelight revealing the thick diagonal scars on Jessey's forearms, appearing uncomfortably bright. Daryl's gossip of suicide rang through his mind again. Jessey was strange, but was she capable of doing something that drastic?

"Hey...Jessey?"

"Yes?"

"Look, I know it ain't my business, aaaright, but I couldn't help but notice that your arms there look like it went through a really rough time."

He pointed his finger. Jessey didn't look down. It was unnecessary to home in on where he meant. She had seen others point in the past year and had always given them a bogus explanation. The rumors had spread around town anyway. Though her smile looked sad, she was pleased to tell the truth about it.

"And you want to know how I got it," she said. "What do you think? Was it a suicide attempt?"

"I don't think so," Willy said. "You don't seem like the type to me. Was it an accident or something?"

"Or something," Jessey said. She looked at her scars. She made a tight fist and watched her forearm muscles budge. "This little accident came from an evil entity called 'Bloody Mary.' She gave us a handful last year and put me in the hospital. We'll leave it at that. Are you ready now?"

Willy bent over and picked up his boxing gloves. He slipped them on and got into fighting position: chin down, fists up, knees bent, and standing sideways. "Let's do this."

After slipping into her gloves, Jessey came at him with a battle cry and threw fast punches. Willy felt soft wind hit his face as he blocked her assaults.

She went for a kick.

Willy dodged with a grunt.

Another series of punches. All of them intercepted.

At one last attempt, Jessey bent herself low to the ground and spun with her leg out to sweep Willy's.

He jumped in time to avoid collision and Jessey's leg had done a three-sixty. Both poised for battle, but after a pause of staring at each other and waiting for one to make the next move, they were laughing.

CHAPTER 23

October 29

"Fifty-two inches," Cindy Daniels said as she coiled up her measuring tape. She had scaled Willy from the top of his back to between his calf and ankle, ten inches from Huford House's floor. Unlike his physical training with Jessey Sassacus in the basement, Willy and Cindy were in the attic.

"You look to be about a medium, I'd say."

The second floor and attic windows were the only windows in the house that weren't boarded up and it was nice to see the sun shine through the ancient glass. The solar rays, however, didn't help the temperature. Early October was an Indian summer extension, but now it was cold. They can see traces of their breath, leaving Willy to wish that he hadn't taken off his *Oakland Raiders* jacket when he came up the attic stairs. According to Cindy, it was necessary for the jacket to stay off for proper measurements to be made. Because she had measured Jessey last year and Marty Takahoshi the year before, she had come prepared for the chilly atmosphere, dressed in thick tights, a plaid flannel skirt, and a button sweater.

"You making me a suit?" Willy said.

"Something like that," Cindy said. She shoved the tape measure in her sweater pocket and rubbed her hands together, "Do you remember the caribou skin that you took out from your dream with the Pequot Indians?'

"Yeah."

"I need to sew it onto your uniform," she said.

The east attic wall was bare because the wood in that area appeared too weak for anything to stand on. Antique bureaus, hope chests, and desks occupied the other three walls and nearly concealed the slanted roof ceiling. Cindy walked over to the nearest hope chest and parted the double doors. Dust puffed in the air as Willy tilted his head to get a peek at what was behind "door number one." What he saw were yards of dangling black fabric from wire coat hangers. As Cindy looked through them and shifted the ones that wouldn't do to the left, Willy noticed that the black fabrics were actually capes of various sizes. The inside of every cape was a different color. There was green, white, purple, gray, blue (the same kind of cape that Vince Thomason wore in his dream as Willy remembered) and finally, red.

Cindy took out a black and red cape. She extended it to Willy. "See if that fits you."

Willy took hold of the wire hook and held up the cape to the level of his eyes. It was heavy. A single eyebrow rose. "Oh cool, I get to be *Dracula* this year."

"Not really," Cindy said, "that's what all the Colts wear. You're going to wear it this year just like Jessey wore it last year and like Marty before her and so on back."

"I've been thinking about this 'Colt' thing," Willy said. "How about a cooler nickname?"

"Like what?" Cindy said. She didn't look at Willy. She was too busy opening a middle drawer to the bureau next to the hope chest.

"I don't know. How about something like 'Ice-Pick'?"

"How about 'no?'" Cindy laughed as she pulled out a black sweatshirt and a pair of red elbow pads.

"Well 'Colt' sounds stupid, aaaright?" Willy said, "I feel like a veal cutlet."

Cindy laughed harder as she placed the sweatshirt and elbow pads on top of the bureau. "Just try on the cape, okay?"

Willy rolled his eyes and took the cape off the hanger. The cape's weight reminded him of the lead vest he wore the last time he went to the dentist. Dr. Solomon said the lead vest is used when taking teeth X-rays. "A tad heavy, ain't it?"

"You'll get used to the weight," Cindy said. "It could even save your life."

"What do you mean?" Willy said.

"The cape is water-proof, fire-proof, and bullet-proof," Cindy said. "It's also very tough to cut through."

"Bullet-proof? Cut?" Willy said, "What are you saying? Am I gonna to get shot at? Is something out there going to pull a knife on me?"

"No, it's just a precaution," Cindy said. "You can never be too prepared."

Willy tossed the wire hanger to the floor and flipped the cape over his back. Cindy pulled out the bottom drawer and took out black sweatpants and red kneepads. When she collected the sweats and pads and turned around, she saw Willy. His cape covered his whole body with the exception of his lower legs. She smiled and approached him. She tilted her head, circled him, then nodded.

"Take these." She handed Willy the clothes and pads, "What shoe size are you? Six or seven?"

"Seven," Willy said. "How did you know?"

"I pay attention," Cindy said. She strode to the other side of the attic where another hope chest stood on her right. Ahead of her was a desk. She approached the desk and opened a top drawer. Willy saw her sorting through some papers and pulled out a thin box, about a foot at length. Cindy removed the cover and the tissue-layered inside. She pulled out a red belt and a pair of long red leathery gloves. They were also fire and waterproof. She then went to the hope chest and opened its double doors. It was filled with different size pairs of combat boots that had been spray-painted a variety of colors. Her fingers hooked a pair of red combat boots and took them out.

"Go downstairs and try this stuff on," she said.

Willy obliged as he added the gloves, belt, and boots to his new outfit. He galloped down the stairs as loud and hollow noise echoed around the attic.

It was getting close. The most dangerous night of the year was just around the corner. Cindy wanted to tell him that it wouldn't be scary, that the nightmare would be over starting November first. She prayed that Willy Hynes would luck out and not go through the traumatizing things that she went through and still does to this day. The evil that the Pniese deal with can get locked up, but the memories were always free.

Five minutes later, the loud hollow thumps echoed throughout the attic again. Willy Hynes came up the stairs. He was wearing the black sweats, the red elbow and kneepads, and the red boots on his feet. The red belt was secured around his waist and the leather gloves stretched halfway up his forearms. His cape flapped below his spine. He looked like a cross between a pro wrestler and a superhero. When Cindy Daniels gave a "thumbs up," déjà vu hit him once again.

"You're going to need this," Cindy said.

She held up a red raccoon-style mask, similar to the one that Vince wore in his dream.

Willy took the mask. At first, he wondered why there was no string or elastic attached to both sides of it. When he felt it, he realized that the inside of it was gluey. White slits covered Willy's brown eyes as he stuck it to his face, above the nose.

"You look good…" Cindy said nodding, "…Colt."

CHAPTER 24

October 31

Bill Swifburg put his father's green Ford Mustang in reverse and backed in towards Huford House's rear entrance. Vince Thomason waved his hands, indicating that Bill could keep coming without hitting the stone foundation. Willy stood beside him. He looked into the distant woods and let his mind wander. It was the big day and soon-to-be the big night, yet he felt calm. It was the kind of calm he didn't trust. His thoughts were of past Halloweens and all the monsters he saw. He wondered which ones were real and which weren't. Sure, some were obvious. He could tell if a monster was really an eight-year-old in a plastic mask or a ghost made from bed sheets and he was sure that there was no actual *Freddy Krueger* in the Netherworld. Still, he remembered seeing vampires whose fangs looked too authentic and zombies whose stench was too genuine.

Huford House's back door made a rusty crackling as it pulled open. Cindy Daniels and Jessey Sassacus came out. Jessey had her grip on Marty Takahoshi's arm as she led him out. Willy acknowledged them with a nod and a smile.

"Hey Willy, pay attention!" Vince said, clapping his hands.

Willy broke from his daydreaming and heard the Ford's engine subside. Bill Swifburg got out of car and joined the others. He opened the trunk, revealing a large plastic tub. The tub was three-quarters filled with ice.

"Help me grab one end," Vince said.

"What are we having, a party or something?" Willy said.

"No, you're looking at one of our best weapons."

"Ice?" Willy said, "What are we gonna to do? Fix the bad guys margaritas if they get out of line?"

"Use your head," Vince said. "This ice has been blessed at Saint Roland's Cathedral. Father O'Hill is an ally of the Pniese. Once this ice melts…"

"It becomes holy water, I get it," Willy said. "But why bless it as ice?"

"Easier to deal with," Bill said. "If this were melted, my old man's trunk would be flooded. As ice, it's easier to carry."

The ends of the tub were looped and tied with thick ropes. Bill counted with a one, two, three, and together, they heaved and pulled the ice out of the Ford's trunk. The thawing ice was still heavy, even with three of them handling the tub. They took limp baby steps towards the house. Grinding their teeth, the three struggled through the entrance and laid the tub next to the doorway on the right. Bill rubbed his hands together, trying to warm them up. Vince wiped moisture from his palms onto his jeans while Willy inspected his own hands. He saw rope marks leftover from the pulling.

"It's getting about that time," Cindy said. "I think we should change and get our weapons together and so on."

Marty felt his Braille watch. "Four-thirty. Sounds like a plan to me."

For Willy, the next half-hour felt like a montage from an action movie. The boys were in an upstairs bedroom while the girls changed across the hall. He saw himself and the other guys slip into black sweats, step into combat boots, snap on belts, squeeze into elbow and knee pads, pull on gloves, tie on capes, and stick raccoon-style masks on their faces, which white out their eyes.

Willy looked at a mirror on the wall. It was cracked at the bottom and coated with dust, but he still saw himself as Cindy Daniels did two days ago. Willy wasn't that big, yet the outfit gave him a sense of power. He had seen others, including Vince, wear this kind of outfit during his trick-or-treating years (and later, just his tricking years) and always wondered whom exactly they were supposed to be dressed as. They didn't look like any superhero he had seen before. He also never believed that he would one day wear the same kind of costume. On his right shoulder he noticed that Cindy Daniels had kept her word. She sewed on the patch of caribou skin he pulled from his dream.

"Lookin' pretty good," Bill Swifburg said. Willy saw Bill's reflection behind him. He about-faced and examined his ally. Despite his good nature, Bill looked somewhat intimidating in his outfit. It was nearly the same as his own, but Bill's mask, inside cape, belt, elbow and knee pads, combat boots, and gloves were green as opposed to Willy's red.

"Bring it on, I'm ready," Willy said. He cracked his knuckles, "I'm still not big on the nickname 'Colt', but I'll go along with it."

"Nice to have your approval," Bill said. "As for me, tonight, the name is 'Jadeite.'"

"Wow, your nickname is no improvement," Willy the Colt said.

Willy glanced past "Jadeite" and noticed Vince and Marty. They were straightening their costumes and adjusting their capes. Like the rest, Marty wore the black sweats and his mask, belt, elbow pads, kneepads, combat boots, gloves, and inner cape were gray.

"Call me 'Moonbeam,'" Marty said, sensing Willy the Colt's staring.

Vince looked as he did in Willy's dream over a month ago. The mask, belt, elbow and kneepads, combat boots, gloves, and inner cape were blue. His dark attire seemed to enhance his normally stern expression. In the faded sunshine, his sable figure stood out like a serpent in a flower garden.

"And you are?" Willy the Colt said.

"Twilight," Vince said.

CHAPTER
25

Huford House's basement had come to life as it did the night Willy Hynes had entered it over a month ago and made his first step into becoming Colt. White candles surrounded the room: some on the walls, held by tarnished brass candlesticks and some on the tables that held Pniese weapons. Twilight and Colt's footsteps echoed as they went down the stairs. The sulking dust coughed in the air and fluttered down to the floor.

"Not for nothing, Vince," Colt said, "but someone should go medieval on this place with lemon *Pledge*."

"It's 'Twilight,'" Vince said. "Once these suits are put on, we go by our aliases. You got to get into the habit of doing that. No real names until Halloween is over and what not. You understand, *Colt*?"

"Sorry," Colt said, then bent his first and middle fingers together indicating quotation, "'Twilight.'"

Twilight approached the tables with Colt behind him and picked up a walkie-talkie. He turned it on. Static. He held down the "talk" button. "Moonbeam? Can you hear me? Over."

Twilight released the "talk" button.

"Loud and clear, Twilight. Over," the walkie-talkie said in Marty's voice.

"Thank you. Out," Twilight said. He handed the walkie-talkie to his protégé, "Put that on your belt."

Colt took the walkie-talkie and saw that the back of it had a latch. Though it was difficult with gloves on, he managed to obey Twilight's order and slid it on his red belt.

Twilight grabbed another object from the table. When he turned around, he displayed a pair of handcuffs with the keys still in its slot.

"These handcuffs were specially made," he said. "Solid silver. That means if you have to, you can cuff any supernatural and they won't have the power to break free. Silver is very powerful like that."

"Too bad it doesn't work on ghosts," Colt said, half-serious and half-joking.

Twilight reached back to the table with one hand and seized a small plastic squeezable tube that was filled with some kind of blue gel.

"This is ectoplasm," he held the tube up next to his dark chin. "You just squirt some of this on the cuffs and it will hold ghosts, phantoms, spirits, and what not. Just don't squirt too much. This stuff is hard to come by."

"Aaaright." Colt smirked as Twilight handed him the cuffs and tube, "So what else do I get?"

Twilight handed him a red squirt gun.

"You got to be kidding."

"Take it," Twilight said, "It may not be an Uzi, but when you fill it with holy water, you got yourself a potent weapon."

Colt didn't think of it that way, but he accepted the "childish" toy. Twilight took one last object from the table behind him and turned to Colt. A grappling hook and cord was in his grip.

"Just in case we need to go in high places, you're going to need this," he said. "The hook can hold up to 250 pounds and the cable is made from steel. You shouldn't have to worry about it snapping on you."

"I hope not," Colt said, "that wouldn't be very healthy for me."

More echoing footsteps were heard coming down to the basement. Twilight looked up and Colt turned around to see Cindy Daniels in her outfit. Like the boys, she wore the black sweats. The outside of her cape was black as well. Yet, her elbow and kneepads, belt, combat boots, gloves, inside cape, and raccoon-style mask were off-white. Her eyes were whited out as well once the mask was on. There was no trace of her former sky blues.

"Prayer time will be in five minutes," she said.

"We'll be ready," Twilight said.

Cindy walked past them and made her way over to the table. Next to a three-stemmed candlestick were a white bow, a quiver of arrows, some standard and some with silver broadheads, and a pair of white *Roller Blades*. She smiled at Colt as she strapped her quiver to her back.

"You nervous?" she said.

"A little," he said, "but I'll be okay."

"Only if you do what I say," Twilight said.

Colt looked to Twilight and pouted his thick lips, giving him an "I know, I know" look. Cindy pulled up a decrepit-looking chair and started to undo the laces on her boots.

"So what's your pet name for tonight?" Colt said.

"Angel," Cindy said. She slipped off a boot and revealed a white sock-covered foot. She took hold of one of the *Roller Blades* and started to loosen its laces.

"Where'd you guys come up with these names?" Colt said.

"These are names that have been used for ages," Cindy the Angel said. "They go with the colors we wear and they can be used for both boys and girls. Also, this is what the supernaturals know us by. You understand, right?"

"Yeah, I can understand," Colt said. "So, what's with the skates?"

"It helps me get around faster," Angel said. She put on her second skate, "We all have our little means of transportation. Jadeite uses a skateboard, believe it or not."

Colt laughed. "I gotta get a picture of that!"

Twilight cleared his throat as Colt and Angel turned to him. He reached for a small jewelry box from the table and opened it. Inside was a collection of badges, made from silver and formed into seven-pointed stars. A piece of amber, shaped like a pumpkin, took up the center. One word was engraved on each star's point. Colt leaned in closer to read each word.

"Wisdom, courage, justice, patience, hope, faith, charity."

"Those are the seven Cardinal virtues and the code that all good people live by," Twilight said. He took one of the badges out and placed the box back on the table, "This star is a symbol of authority and with it, holds tremendous responsibility. As your trainer, I hereby appoint you as a member of the Pniese."

Twilight stepped forward and pinned the badge on Colt's right pectoral. Colt smiled and turned to Angel who gave him a wink.

Twilight took hold of the jewelry box again, picked out a silver star, and extended it to Angel.

"Your badge."

She took it and fumbled to pin it on her sweatshirt. "Thank you."

As Twilight did the same, the basement stairs were getting trampled as the rest of the Pniese came down. Jadeite came first with his arm around Moonbeam's as he guided Moonbeam down to Huford House's catacombs. Jessey Sassacus followed with her hair in a braided ponytail and in her Pniese outfit. It was the same as the others. She wore the black cape and sweats with the caribou patch. Her mask, inside cape, boots, belt, gloves, elbow and kneepads were a different color from the rest. In her case, the color was purple.

"Everyone get their weapons, badges, and walkie-talkies," Angel said. "It's almost game time."

CHAPTER 26

Everyone huddled together like football players getting ready to discuss their strategies. They were on one knee, their heads down, and their right arms extended. The tips of their fingers touched the warrior that was across from them. Their thumbs scraped the heel of the warrior's hand next to them. In Colt's case, his fingertips were touching Jadeite's and his thumb was scraping the back of Twilight's hand. From an aerial view, the Pniese's extended arms resembled a kind of wheel.

Everyone had their weapons and supplies attached to their belts or backpacks. No one was without his or her badge, walkie-talkie, or holy water-filled squirt gun. Jadeite's weapon was a slingshot and unlike the others, a leather pouch took up the side of his belt. Colt didn't know what was in it. While Moonbeam's right arm was extended, his left hand held a staff that was approximately the same height as he was. The staff, Moonbeam told Colt, was made of silver. Jessey Sassacus's weapon resembled a whip. It had a handle, but instead of leather ribbons, the strip part was made of purple wampum. Colt learned from Jessey during their hand-to-hand combat training that wampum are polished beads made from clam shells and were used by her ancestors as money and ceremonial pledges. Purple wampum was the rarest kind.

"Everyone clear your minds," Angel said, starting the group prayer. "May we all be safe tonight. May the innocent be protected and the wicked brought to justice. May we all practice good judgment and never abuse the authority and power that have been passed onto us. May our Colt learn well and may his trainer move on to happiness and prosperity. Teamwork, discipline, and trust. This is the way of the Pniese and this is what we will enforce on this night."

Everyone rose to his and her feet. The sun was almost down. Halloween night was creeping up. They could already hear Mrs.

Beaumont's scary sound effects CD up the street as she waited for trick-or-treaters. Jadeite began blowing out the candles in the basement.

Twilight clapped Angel's shoulder. "Good prayer."

"That's the easy part," she said. "I just hope I can be half the leader you were last year. I don't know what to expect. I really don't."

"No one knows what to expect," Twilight said. "All anyone can do is their best."

"Thanks," Angel said. She took his hand, "You might want to tell that to your Colt."

Twilight didn't reply. He looked over at Colt who was talking to Jessey Sassacus.

"I didn't catch your name for tonight," Colt said to Jessey. "Let me guess...'Violet Vixen'?"

"No," Jessey said, trying not to smile at Colt's humor. "Tonight, you can call me 'Specter.'"

"Specter?" Colt said, "Why do they call you that?"

Jessey the Specter took hold of her wampum whip, one hand on each end. She started to jump rope with it. Colt was ready to snicker, but his eyes nearly dried out as they protruded from their sockets. With every skip Jessey the Specter made with her wampum whip, she became more transparent. Colt stuck out his finger and touched her arm.

It went straight through.

"Neat, huh?" Specter said, "I can go through walls and even make myself invisible if I wanted to."

"Damn." That was the only thing Colt could say. When he said it, he stretched it as far as he could. Then he wondered why he was stuck with a lousy squirt gun.

CHAPTER
27

Angel had gone ahead of the others on her *Roller Blades*. The annual Halloween party at Sleepy Owl town square starts within an hour and that's where most of the action takes place for both the living and supernaturals alike. Jadeite soon followed on his skateboard. On the way to the party, he will make a quick patrol of the streets that cross his path.

That left Moonbeam, Specter, Twilight, and Colt, still in Huford House. They were staring at a map of Sleepy Owl laid out on an ancient dinner table in the kitchen. The map was filled with different colored circles in different areas. Each color indicated a place to patrol and what kind of supernatural would most likely be encountered there.

"How about me and Colt make a sweep of the north and west?" Twilight said. He pointed to those areas on the map, "It's much farther away and we can get there quicker."

"That's fine by me," Moonbeam said. "I need to stop by Lake Black Feather and pick up my ride."

"After that, we can get to the east-side by six-thirty," Specter said.

"Ride?" Colt said, "What ride?"

"You'll see in a little while," Twilight said. "Go to the back yard. I'll be out in a minute. Don't touch anything. And don't wander either."

"'Don't touch anything, don't wander either'?" Colt said, "What am I, three?"

"Git," Twilight said, pointing his finger.

Colt walked away, muttering too low for the others to understand.

"Ease up on him, Vince," Specter said.

"The Pniese can't afford to mess around during the crucial hours," Twilight said.

"The Pniese is from my heritage more than anybody else's," Specter said. "Even the ancient warriors will tell you that conviction is important too."

"Sometimes, he's too overconfident. That can seal your fate on a night like this."

"No argument there," Moonbeam said, "but I believe Willy will know what to do when the time is right. Don't you believe that? Isn't that why he was chosen?"

"Yeah, I know you guys are right and what not," Twilight said. "I've just been looking out for him for so long. It's hard to know when to stop."

Traces of the sun were still seen in the west. It hid behind trees and took its time departing like an actor, refusing to get off stage long after the ovations are over. It was a deep rusty orange and its rays were no longer strong or vivid.

Halloween night was ready to float in with its annual promise of mystery and enchantment. Mrs. Beaumont's scary sound effects CD was louder than ever as were the faint voices of trick-or-treaters getting an early start. Colt looked around Huford House's backyard, which was all forestland. He remembered that Twilight told him that the supernaturals came to this world through the four elements: earth, air, fire, and water. Colt gazed at the somber trees that surrounded him and wondered if a few ghosts and goblins would pop out of the thick trunks and wave "hello," or possibly even attack. It was truly starting to sink in now. On this night, Colt will see creatures that had only existed in his mind, old storybooks, and bad horror movies.

"Let's do this," Twilight said from behind as he shut the back door.

"Aaaright," Colt said.

Twilight lead the way and headed towards the woods. Colt stuck close behind, his holy water squirt gun drawn as he looked around like a cop going into a combat zone. A woodpile that was held together by two strong oaks was up ahead. Though it was dark out, Colt saw that the lumber was decayed and piled high, almost the same height as he was. Its length had to be at least fifteen feet as they drew closer to it. Their boots snapped on dead leaves and fallen branches.

Twilight and Colt circled the woodpile and came to a huge bulge. A heavy plastic canvas, probably black or navy blue, covered something huge. It was the size of a pool table or maybe a bunch of old couches. One thing Colt realized about the Pniese so far was that you never knew anything for sure.

"Put that away..." Twilight said, regarding Colt having his squirt gun drawn, "...and give me a hand with this."

As Colt placed his squirt gun back in the holster attached to his belt, he saw Twilight bend down and reach for one of the canvas corners. It made a rumbling when he began to pull it off. Colt took another corner and joined in. Once he saw the steel bumper, he recognized what was under the canvas. It had knobs on each end of its front bumper called bullets and fins made of chrome in the back. Its headlights were circular and had a visor over each one. Its colors were black and white and it had an eerie glow to it that couldn't possibly come from *Turtle Wax*. It was a 1957 Chevy Bel Air.

"I was hoping for a Ferrari," Colt said.

"If you got a couple hundred-thousand lying around, I'll see what I can do," Twilight said. "Fold the canvas and put it off to the side."

The canvas made a deep crackling sound with every fold. Colt heard a faint jingle as Twilight took a set of keys out of his pocket and unlocked the trunk. The canvas was given one last fold over and then Colt dragged it to the other side of the woodpile.

The trunk's inside light shined on more equipment as Colt saw when he re-joined his mentor. "The wetsuits are right there," Twilight pointed at the folded up rubber attire, "One for me and one for you."

Colt gave the wetsuits a quick glance. The thing that attracted his attention the most was a black and blue helmet with a see-through protective visor and a funny-looking cog in the mouth area. He picked it up. "What's this?"

"That's an ultra-modern Breathalyzer for underwater activity," Twilight said. "There's only one of those, unfortunately."

Twilight took the helmet away from Colt and set it back into the trunk beside the First-Aid kit and a stack of wool blankets. He pulled out a pair of diving masks and miniature flashlights. "Take one of each and attach them to the back of your belt."

When Colt sat in the passenger side, he marveled at how different the car's interior looked from what he expected. There were no fuzzy dice dangling from the rear view mirror or one of those ancient knob-turning radios that had a tiny red stick to show what station you were listening to. Everything, except for the door locks, seemed up to date. The shift gear was on the side instead of being attached to the wheel. The seat belts were electric and the mileage was in digital numbers.

"Only fifty-thousand miles?" Colt said.

"We usually only use it on this night," Twilight said. "Besides, this bad boy ain't registered. If we get pulled over in the daytime and what not, there would be a whole lot of explaining to do."

"Have you guys ever been pulled over before?" Colt said, "On Halloween night, I mean?"

"For some odd reason, no," Twilight said. "Then again, the Pniese have allies in the local police and Moonbeam's uncle works for the Registry of Motor Vehicles. As long as we don't drive this at any other time, we should be okay."

Twilight turned the engine over.

"Oh yeah," Twilight pointed to the ashtray, "there's also an extra set of keys in there. You might want to put them in your pocket just in case."

"Just in case of what?"

"Just in case I lose mine by some unlikely bad luck."

After a shifting from "park" to "drive," the '57 Chevy pulled out of the woods, crawling its way to the left side of Huford House. Colt dipped his gloved fingers into the ashtray and pulled out the extra set of keys, while he continued to look around. He noticed details like the CB on the side and the glowing panels that indicated how much gas they had, how fast they were going, and what direction they were heading in. There had to have been crazy gadgets and secret turbo chargers or something around here—Colt was positive about that.

"Did you build all this?"

"Me and my relatives," Twilight said. "They got this car back in the late fifties and over the course of years, gave it a whole bunch of modifications. Coming from a long line of mechanics will do that."

"And what do we call this piece of machinery?" Colt said.

Twilight turned to him as they rolled onto Baykok Avenue. "The car."

"The car?" Colt said, "You mean after all the code names and stuff, you guys ain't got some crazy name for this?"

"What do you want to call it?"

"I don't know," Colt said and looked out the window. "Hey, there's Jes—I mean, Specter and Moonbeam."

Twilight looked to his right and saw them walking along Baykok Avenue, heading for Lake Black Feather. Their capes twisted in the wind as Specter took Moonbeam's arm and guided him. Twilight waved and drove past them.

"That reminds me," Colt said, "Specter showed me this cool little jump rope or whip that can make her like a ghost or even invisible. Do I get one of those too?"

"Nope."

"What about you?"

"Nope."

"Well, why not?"

"That wampum whip has belonged to her ancestors for centuries. It's completely unique," Twilight said. "Each Pniese gets their own specialties. That's the way it is."

"Okay, so what's our specialty?" Colt said.

"This car and the water," Twilight said. He pushed harder on the gas.

Moonbeam and Specter took the unpaved trail that started on Baykok Avenue, crossed La Llorona Avenue, and continued until they arrived at Lake Black Feather somewhere between five and ten minutes after Twilight sped by. Specter saw the nearly full moon rise from the hills on the horizon as they cut through a small section of woods and treaded past an old row boat that had long been the feast of termites. They stopped within ten feet of the lake.

"What time is it?" Specter said.

Moonbeam peeled off three-quarters of his gray glove and felt his Braille watch. "Almost six."

"Any minute now," Specter said.

They gazed at the silver-hued lake.

It first started off with a couple of bubbles. Then it grew to a boil as a section of the lake, about thirty feet from shore, came to life as if it were a giant Jacuzzi tub. The fizzling neither excited nor bored Specter and Moonbeam. They looked on and waited. The water erupted into a monstrous splash and a neighing white stallion ascended to the surface. The leap it made rivaled any show jumper. It galloped on top of the water and headed to shore. It slowed down as it approached Moonbeam and Specter and then stopped and shook off the remaining water from its thin fur.

Moonbeam's gray gloved-fingers stroked between the horse's opal-like eyes. He smiled as the stallion lowered its head.

"Hello, Phantom," Moonbeam said in its ear. "Ready to go to work? "

CHAPTER
28

It won't be long now. The coal that the Devil gave him was almost used up. The flame that kept him bound and forced him to travel for several lifetimes was, at last, coming to a close. It was the end of the long walk and Jack couldn't wait to taste freedom. He held the metal lantern up to his tangerine eyes, dancing with adrenaline. He watched that one special piece of coal struggle to glow in the last of its flickering. He couldn't help himself. He had to laugh as he walked along Raven River and crossed into Sleepy Owl, Connecticut. The cursed coal choked its last breath of red heat then succumbed.

"I'm free!" he said in his graveled voice to the All Hallow's Eve sky.

He set the lantern to the ground and opened its glass door. His scarred green hand seized the cursed piece of coal. He took it out and felt how fragile it was. What was once blistering and binding was now an aged chunk of white soot. Jack's deformed grin stretched wider and almost occupied his entire lower face. Brown teeth, never acquainted with toothpaste, peeked out from his lips.

"Nothing can stop me now."

He turned back to Raven River, whose tranquil dark water flashed with points of moonlit reflections. He wound up and threw. The coal flew into the autumn air as white specks of it chipped off and left a trail of dust behind like a comet. It bounced off a wooden beam that supported a small ramshackle bridge then plopped into the water. The cursed coal made almost no splash, but the wet popping noise that it made was loud enough for Jack's keen ears to hear. He could almost feel it descend to the frigid bottom.

The illumination color inside Jack's lantern changed from crimson to turquoise. Its mesmerizing power was still intact and its owner was no longer confined. His slimy tongue licked his lips.

He was thirsty.

CHAPTER
29

By six-thirty, Sleepy Owl town square stirred with electricity and excitement as it did every Halloween night. Tiny saffron lights were rigged up on nearby maple trees. Jack o'lanterns expressed themselves with toothless smiles and horrified grins. Inside the town's gazebo was Spider Web, a rock band that few persons knew were from the Netherworld. The band consisted of Lockjaw, a zombie and the lead singer, Ribs, a ghoul, and Eliza, a vampire, on guitars, and on the drums, Hermy the hunchback. A large crowd dressed up in such outfits as *Darth Vader*, pirates, nurses, *Tarzan*, clowns, cowboys, *Leatherface, Austin Powers,* and *Iron Man* surrounded the gazebo. Every year, Spider Web sang the same songs like *Ghostbusters, Monster Mash, Thriller, Purple People Eater, Werewolves of London, I Put a Spell on You,* and anything related to Halloween. Though the young townsfolk enjoyed hearing such familiar tunes, they asked every now and again if the band knew any song from *Godsmack* or *Hannah Montana* or *Train* only to get a decline.

In front of the gazebo were three tables put together lengthwise and covered in black vinyl cloth. It was a long buffet with treats donated by volunteers and persons in the town committee. At one end were stacks of *Styrofoam* plates, cups, and plastic dinnerware. Next to that was a large bowl of red fruit punch. A chunk of ice shaped like a hand floated in it. Orange-frosted cupcakes, candy corn, pumpkin shaped chocolate lollipops, *M&M's* brownies, candy apples, marshmallow ghosts, and fried dough took up the rest of the space. A double-sided line had been forming for the past twenty minutes and showed no signs of slowing as both humans and unsuspected supernaturals waited to get their goodies.

Less than an eighth of a mile up the street was the old Meriweather house. It was built in the early twentieth century, but hadn't been lived in since the 1950s when millionaire Ted Meriweather went bankrupt and sold it. No one had bought it because although Ted Meriweather was wealthy, he was also stingy with his money and never made any kind of repairs to his home. As a result, the paint had chipped, the shudders barely hung on, and the door made an awful creak whenever its knob was turned and pushed. Eventually, the town of Sleepy Owl bought it, but never made the necessary repairs until ten years ago when someone suggested that it be fixed up to look like a haunted mansion for their annual Halloween celebration. Since that time, the Meriweather house had become a hit and has entertained thousands of persons willing to pay admission to go in and see if they could "survive" the terror. Contrary to what may be assumed, the supernaturals never got involved with the actual haunted house show, but most loved to check it out. It's always ironic when a teen-ager in a vampire outfit actually frightens a real vampire. Throughout all of this, the Pniese looked on like chaperones at a school dance.

Jadeite leaned up against a nearby telephone pole. One green boot rested on top of his skateboard, sliding it a few inches back and forth. Angel glided on her *Roller Blades*. She decided to leave the area and do another sweep of all the nearby streets. Moonbeam and Specter were halfway across town, doing a check on Sleepy Owl Cemetery as they rode on Phantom, the white stallion.

Twilight sat in his black and white '57 Chevy with his protégé, Colt. The vehicle rested along with several others in the *Sleepy Owl Trust* bank parking lot where they had a full view of town square and its entire hubbub. Twilight looked on. He watched a woman dressed as a ballerina instruct a group of costumed kids on pinning the tail on the werewolf. Each child got a piece of brown paper that was cut into the shape of a shaggy tail with a tiny pin in it. They were told that the winner was the one who could pin the tail on the picture of the werewolf stapled to the maple tree in front of them. The ballerina spun the first child who was dressed as *Harry Potter* 'round and 'round. The other kids laughed as the little boy with the painted lightning bolt on his head aimed the paper tail too high, ready to pin it near the werewolf's head.

A tune started to hum inside Twilight's mouth. It was a tune that was vaguely familiar to Colt. After five minutes of it, Colt could stand it no longer.

"Aaaright, what is that?"

"What's what?" Twilight said.

"That song you're humming," Colt said. "What is it?"

Twilight shifted in the driver's seat. He was hesitant to reply.

"Come on," said Colt, "give it up."

"It's '*Rubber Duckie*,'" Twilight said.

Colt laughed. "*Rubber Duckie?*"

"Yes, *Rubber Duckie*."

"Of all the songs in the world, why are you humming '*Rubber Duckie*?' Don't get me wrong, I liked it. Then I turned four."

"I was over my Aunt Wilma's house the other night," Twilight said. "Her two-year-old daughter was watching *Sesame Street*. I figured I'd sit down and play with the kid a little. All of sudden, *Ernie* came on in the bathtub and he was singing…"

Twilight started to sing, "'Rubber Duckie, you're the one. You make bath time lots of fun...'"

"You are so sad," Colt said.

"It's just a little catchy, that's all."

"Whatever floats your boat. For an encore, how about '*C is for Cookie*'?"

"I'm not gonna sing '*C is for Cookie*.'"

"Don't let me stop you. By all means, go ahead. I don't mind."

"You made your point," Twilight said. "It's out of my head as of right now."

The car was silent for a moment. All that was heard was the constant chatter around town square and the horror sound effects coming from the Meriweather house. Twilight looked on, tight-lipped.

"Rubber Duckie, you're the one." he sang in a mumbling voice, "You make bath time lots of fun…."

His voice wasn't low enough to escape Colt's ears. Colt chuckled in his throat, but he couldn't contain it. His laughter filled the car.

"You weak, weak man!" Colt slapped his hands together.

"Hey, don't lose your focus," Twilight said.

"You're the one singing '*Rubber Duckie!*'" Colt laughed.

"That's different. I can sing and not lose my focus."

"Well I can laugh and not lose my focus, aaaright?"

"All I'm saying—"

Twilight's sentence was cut off when he heard a loud pounding. It came from the other side of his driver's door.

Colt took out his holy water squirt gun. "What was that?"

"I don't know," Twilight said.

The pounding again. Twilight felt the door's vibration on his leg, which was pressed against it. He looked out his window and saw no one.

"It's probably some kid scrunched down," he said. "I'm gonna open it."

"I'm ready," Colt said. He aimed his squirt gun in the space between Twilight's arm and lap. His finger was on the plastic trigger.

Twilight wrapped his blue-gloved fingers around the handle and opened the driver's door.

A tiny head peeked. Then its body, all two and a half feet of it, stepped out from behind the driver's door. Though it was toddler height, it was no child. Its red beard and the wrinkles under its green eyes made it look as if its age was close to forty.

"Oh, Twilight!" the short man said, "Saints preserve us!"

Colt noticed that the short man was dressed in a vest, short pants, stockings, and a derby with a four-leaf clover sticking out of it. The whole outfit was green except for the black shoes and the strap on his hat, both fastened with brass buckles. Traces of shaving cream were found in his beard, shoulders, and the top of his derby. Twilight recognized the dwarf.

"Hey, Darby," he said. "What's going on?"

"Me gold 'tis what's going on!" the little man said, "Two wicked scoundrels went and took it from me grip! You got to arrest them, you do!"

"Now take it easy," Twilight said. "Just tell me what happened, when and where it happened, and what the suspects look like."

"I told ya, I did!" Darby said, "I was walking down the street, heading for the forest to hide me pot o'gold for the night, when all of a sudden—"

"Wait a second," Colt said, "why would you bring your gold over into our world? Why don't you keep it in your world?"

"Do ya think I'm daft, do you?" Darby said, "It can be stolen just as easily on the Other Side! No self-respecting leprechaun keeps his gold in one place for too long, me lad. I always hide me gold in the forests on Halloween."

"Just out of curiosity," Colt said with a huge smile, "Can you do me a favor and say, 'ooh those kids! They're always after me *Lucky Charms!*'"

"Oh, like I've never heard that one before," Darby groaned, then turned to Twilight. "Tis that the best Colt you could find?"

"He'll be okay," Twilight said. "At least I think he will. So spill it."

"I was heading east, toward Raven River," Darby said. "I was just ready to cut across someone's house and head into the woods, when these two ruffians went and came along and smothered me good with shaving cream! Then, they took me gold! One had a painted face like a skeleton and he shoved me down. The other one was dressed like…"

"Like what?" Twilight said.

"You know," said Darby, "those guys with the swords."

Darby put one tiny fist on top of the other and made a sweeping motion, imitating a swordsman cutting through something.

"A musketeer?" Twilight said.

"No, not a musketeer," Darby said.

"*Zorro?*"

"No."

"A *Jedi?*"

"Na-uh," Darby shook his head.

"A pirate?"

"If it was a pirate, I would've said so."

"A ninja?" Colt said.

Darby snapped his stubby fingers and pointed at the protégé. "That's it, lad!" He turned to Twilight, "Looks like he's got half a brain after all!"

Colt had no idea how to take that remark.

"All right, we'll get on it," Twilight said. "You just stay near town square, have a glass of punch and what not. As soon as we get the gold, we'll let you know."

"And don't you be thinking of taking none!" Darby pointed at Colt.

"I won't," said Colt, "but only if you say 'they're magically delicious.'"

Twilight glared at Colt.

"Well he started it," Colt said.

After Twilight made his promise to Darby the leprechaun, he shut his car door and picked up his walkie-talkie. "Attention all units, be on the look out for two kids. One has his face painted like a dead guy and the other is dressed like a ninja. They've stolen a pot of gold and were last seen on the east side of town, probably on Sunshine Avenue, the street that's closest to Raven River."

"How do you know they're really kids?" Colt said.

"Most supernaturals can tell who's human and who isn't," Twilight said. "Fasten your seat belt. We got a problem to solve."

CHAPTER 30

Donnelly's Bar and Grill was open like any other restaurant pub on Halloween night. It was located on Main Street's east-end and far enough from downtown Sleepy Owl where most were attending the annual Halloween party. A few of the regulars had come for a bite and a drink. The evening news and the Husky football game were on the dual televisions above the bar. Fred Donnelly was behind the bar as usual. He dunked dirty glasses in a tub of warm, soapy water. Fred was dressed like Elvis Presley with a sparkling white jumpsuit and a red silk scarf that his wife, Dolores, made for him. His graying red hair was tucked under a jet-black wig that had an exaggerated 1950s Elvis haircut look, complete with sideburns. Fred didn't look like the Elvis of the fifties though. He looked more like the Elvis of the late seventies with his expanded tummy and sweaty forehead.

"Here you go, Roj," he said to Mr. Crussman, a regular customer.

Roger Crussman wasn't dressed in a costume because his job at Sleepy Owl High School didn't permit him to do so. Not that he ever liked Halloween. He thanked Fred Donnelly for his beer and then went on with his annual Halloween speech.

"There's something ain't right with this town."

"Here we go again," Fred Donnelly said. He winked at Wanda, a waitress who knew what would be said next. She heard Roger Crussman's conspiracy theories for the last five years like Fred Donnelly had.

"No, I mean it, Fred," Roger said. "This town is spooked. Every year, I'm more and more convinced of it."

"What did you see this year?" Wanda said, "Another killer clown? Or is it *Frankenstein* this time?"

"If I tell youze," said Roger, "will you promise to keep an open mind?"

"Sure," Wanda said.

"Yeah, all right," Fred said.

Roger pushed his beer aside and leaned closer to the bar. "On the way over here, I looked up at the sky…and I'll bet ten years of my life that I saw a witch on a broomstick."

Wanda smiled. She laughed as quietly as she could through her nose. Fred Donnelly rolled his bloodshot eyes and threw his cleaning rag over his shoulder. Roger felt humiliated as usual. He wondered, like he does every year, why he tells these stories to Fred, Wanda, and anyone else that will listen. Then in his mind, he answered his own question: because someone has to believe him sooner or later. Someone has just got to believe him. Sleepy Owl may be a small town, but what's going on is too massive for only him to believe.

"Roj, Roj, Roj," Fred Donnelly said. "It's Halloween night. Of course you're going to see all kinds of ghosts and goblins out there. That's all part of the fun. You should dress up yourself sometime and try to fit in."

Roger waved Fred off. "Are you kidding? I'm too old to play such nonsense."

"What do you mean? I'm seven years older than you and I still get dressed up. Look Roj, if you saw a monster on any other night, I'd take you seriously, but this whole 'Sleepy Owl-is-haunted-only-on-Halloween-night' jazz is getting old."

"I should sell the house and move away before it's too late," Roger said.

"That's getting old too," Fred Donnelly said.

"Well what about the Monster cops?" Roger said.

"What about them?" Fred said, then turned to Wanda. "You got some business on table four." She nodded to Fred and strode over to her new customers.

"Don't you find it strange that a bunch of kids are wearing the same costumes every year?" Roger said, "I mean what kid does that? And those things they carry around. I saw one of them last year. She was carrying a bow and arrow."

"So what?" Fred Donnelly said, "They're just kids having a good time, that's all. Honestly Roj, either move away from here or stop with these cover-up theories. You sound like that filmmaker, the guy that made *JFK*. James Cameron."

"It's Oliver Stone," Wanda said. She approached the bar with her round cocktail tray, "and I need three *7-ups* and a *Pepsi*."

Fred Donnelly poured the drinks with his soda gun and dragged them across the bar's counter to Wanda. After she took them and headed back to table four, Fred saw a man stand next to Roger.

"Happy Halloween," Fred said. "Jeez, I didn't even see you come in"

Roger looked to his left and yelped. The man was smaller than he was: no more than five feet-ten, but his face looked hideous. His nose was turned up and his rough green skin was teemed with wrinkles. He was dressed in a shabby suit and top hat that concealed most of his orange hair. He looked at Roger and curved his disfigured mouth upward in a nauseating smile filled with jagged brown teeth.

"What are you suppose to be?" Roger said, "A vampire or something?"

The green-skinned disfigured man shook his head.

"Say, compadre," Fred said. "That's a great make-up job on your face. Are you new in this area? I don't think I've seen you around here before."

"I travel around quite a bit," the green-skinned disfigured man said.

"Sounds real exciting," Fred said. "You got a name?"

"Jack."

"Well Jack, what can I get you?"

"Voodoo rum. All of it."

"I've never heard of voodoo rum before," Fred said. "But I've got soda, ale, daiquiris, domestic and imported b—"

"I'll just help myself," Jack said.

Jack held up his metal lantern. The luminous turquoise light shined into Fred's eyes. His pupils shrunk to the size of a single piece of confetti. When Wanda the waitress returned to the bar, Jack turned the lantern on her and soon enough, she became as paralyzed as Fred. Roger wailed and hopped off his stool. He tried to run for it, but Jack caught him by the back of the collar and forced him to look into the light.

"Go drown yourselves!" Jack said, "All of you!"

Fred, Wanda, and Roger began to walk out of the bar. Jack turned his attention, lantern first, to Donnelly's remaining customers and staff.

And smiled.

Contrary to popular belief, witches can be boys as well as girls and none of them are evil. The ones who practice magic for wickedness are called warlocks and like the witches, gender doesn't matter. Hazel was among the witches that enjoyed roaming around Sleepy Owl on Halloween night. She was hundreds of years old, but if she were of this world, she would probably pass for an age close to sixty-five with her frizzy gray hair and hooked nose. She was dressed in the outfit associated with witches in our medieval times. A black robe swallowed her body and a triangular black hat pointed at the moon above. When she cackled, it was heard blocks away. Hazel didn't have green skin, but she did display a wart on her chin and had two-inch fingernails. As stated before, she wasn't bad, just high-strung, especially when she rode on her flying broomstick.

"Stop!" Specter said, riding on Phantom, "Hazel, pull over, now!"

Hazel was flying too low. Her broom hovered about three feet from the ground. If any townsfolk saw her, either suspicion or panic could emerge. From the look of her smile, which was missing several lower teeth, she didn't care.

"Fast as fast can be," she said, "you'll never catch me! Ah hee hee hee heeeee!"

Fortunately for Specter, the chase was on Dumont Drive, one of the newer streets in Sleepy Owl. All of the houses were still being built and the few that were complete weren't sold or occupied. That was good, Specter thought, if no one is around, a cover-up or explanation won't be necessary.

Hazel rode her broomstick at full speed. Specter and Phantom reared close behind. They were heading towards Dumont Drive's dead end. At the dead end, huge piles of plywood were stacked as high as five feet. Countless bricks, two by fours, and wheelbarrows littered the yards.

Specter smirked as she took out her walkie-talkie. "She's moving in! Make your move before she goes any higher!"

Moonbeam sprung from behind one of the stacks of plywood. Using his silver staff, he pole-vaulted his way to the end of the street. By the time Hazel realized what was going on, Moonbeam had twirled his staff and pointed it in her direction. There wasn't enough time or space for Hazel to fly higher. The silver end of Moonbeam's staff would have poked her in the face if she didn't stomp the brakes on her broomstick.

The broomstick made a screeching sound as it slowed to a halt.

Moonbeam's staff came within a foot of hitting her. Phantom neighed and slowed down himself. They had Hazel trapped.

She smiled sheepishly. "Was I going too fast, dearies?"

Moonbeam pointed his silver staff away from her and walked closer. "Let's see that license of yours."

"Right," Hazel said. She scoured her robe pockets.

Specter got off of Phantom and walked over to Moonbeam. She rested her elbow on his shoulder. "Nice work."

Moonbeam stuck out his hand. Specter slapped him five.

"Ah, here it is!" Hazel said. She extended her license to Moonbeam. Moonbeam had no trouble reading it as it was in Braille.

"Is this Hoover Harley of yours still registered?" Specter said.

"Of course," Hazel said. "Twilight told me that it's good for another three years. Would I lie to you, dearie?"

Specter and Moonbeam looked at each other.

"Naaaaah," they said together.

Moonbeam handed back Hazel's flying broomstick license. "Everything looks good on paper. Why don't you tell us why you didn't pull over when we asked you to."

"Oh I'm sorry, dearie," Hazel said. "Every time I have one of those chocolate cupcakes and candy apples at the town square, the sugar just makes me a little hyper. I do love Halloween treats, don't you?"

"More than life itself," Moonbeam said. "And just how many cupcakes and candy apples did you eat?"

"Oh, two or three," Hazel said, looking up at the clear sky.

"Hazel…"

"Seven…each…" she said. "I'm not proud. Gluttony is such a terrible thing. I couldn't help it."

"You know the rules," Specter said. "If your broomstick is registered, you have to fly high, not low. What if one of the trick-or-treaters or adults saw you up close?"

"I know, dearie, I'm sorry," Hazel said. "But this is a very deserted street."

"That doesn't matter," Specter said. "Anybody could have seen you. Kids cross the streets and go through the woods to take short cuts all the time, you know that."

"Oh please don't write me up, dearie," Hazel said. "If I get another write-up, I won't be able to take my broom with me next Halloween."

Specter turned to Moonbeam. "What do you think?"

"I'd cut her a break," Moonbeam said. "It would mean less paperwork."

"Okay Hazel, you're all set," Specter said. "Just remember what we told you."

"Yes dearie, of course," Hazel said. "Have a Happy Halloween!"

A cackle blew out of her mouth as she and her broomstick hovered higher and zoomed out of sight, beyond the trees, and towards the moon.

"You think we did the right thing?" Specter said.

"She's the least of our worries," Moonbeam said. "Come on, let's go."

Moonbeam held out his gray-gloved hand. Specter took it. She was glad he couldn't see her smile. As Specter guided Moonbeam back to Phantom, she noticed someone walking out of the woods beside the constructed house on her left. It was a man, walking slow but steady towards them. Specter let go of Moonbeam's hand.

"What?" Moonbeam said, "What is it?"

"There's a guy coming this way," Specter said. "He looks familiar."

As the man drew closer, more persons followed from the wood's darkness. They passed the constructed house and headed for Dumont Drive's dead end. Specter and Moonbeam stood in their way.

"Who is it?" Moonbeam said. He tightened his grip on the silver staff.

Specter took a step closer to the leading man, her hand on her magic whip, just in case. As he closed in on her, she figured it out.

"It's Mr. Crussman," she said.

Mr. Roger Crussman took his first step onto Dumont Drive. His face was expressionless. He looked straight ahead at the constructed house across the street and the woods behind it…and beyond.

Specter walked beside her high school acquaintance. "Mr. Crussman? Are you all right?"

Roger Crussman didn't answer or look at her. He kept walking towards the other side of the street. The others behind him were now approaching. One of them was a woman dressed in a waitress outfit. Another one was donned in an Elvis Presley costume. About a dozen more persons followed. All of them were in the same condition. Specter believed that if a car were coming to ram them, they wouldn't have noticed.

"Mr. Crussman! What is it? What's happening?" Specter said.

Roger Crussman kept walking.

"Specter, what is it?" Moonbeam said, hearing all the footsteps as the possessed persons crossed the street.

"They all look dazed," Specter said. She noticed the waitress's nametag: "Donnelly's Bar and Grill - Wanda." She also recognized the Elvis impersonator, Fred Donnelly. Fred and her father, Jay Sassacus, were friends. Whenever the Sassacus's went into *Donnelly's Bar and Grill*, they got a discount. In return, whenever Fred Donnelly and his family went to the casinos in Hartford, Jay Sassacus gave them the same benefit.

"All these people, they're all from *Donnelly's*. Something must have happened there."

"I'm on it," Moonbeam said, taking out his walkie-talkie. "You try to snap them out of it, I'll get backup."

Specter nodded. She ran across the street to catch up to Mr. Crussman, who was already past the constructed house and heading into the woods that lead to Raven River. She snapped her fingers near his ears, but got no response.

"Mr. Crussman, what is it? Hello? Oh God."

She let Mr. Crussman walk past her and approached Wanda the waitress.

"Are you okay? Come on, work with me!"

Specter grabbed Wanda by the biceps and shook her. There was no reaction. When Specter let her go, Wanda followed Roger Crussman, heading into the woods.

"Wake up! Come on, wake up!" Specter said as she approached Fred Donnelly. She didn't know what else to do. She tried shaking, snapping, and yelling to no avail. There was only one other thing she thought of. She slapped Fred Donnelly across the face.

He blinked. His hand rubbed his cheek. "What—what happened?"

"Oh, thank God!" Specter said, slapping her hands together. "Listen, you gotta help me. Just slap anyone who comes along."

And they did. Not knowing for sure why, Fred Donnelly, sweating in his Elvis costume, helped the Monster Cop. More than fourteen persons, all of them valued customers at *Donnelly's Bar and Grill* were slapped back to consciousness with no clear memory of how they got to Dumont Drive. With every one that Donnelly slapped, he offered an apology and promised that their next meal at his Bar and Grill would be on the house.

Specter raced back to Dumont Drive's dead end and approached Moonbeam while all the customers spoke in confusion in the middle of the street.

"What happened here?"

"How did I get here?"

"I remember a bright light."

"I remember not having control of my body."

"Did we leave a tip?"

"Hey Donnelly, are my Buffalo wings ready or what?"

Donnelly shrugged his shoulders, feeling just as bewildered.

"Angel," Moonbeam said into his walkie-talkie, "we got a possible situation at *Donnelly's Bar and Grill*. The people went haywire. We need someone to check it out. Over."

"I'll look into it. Out," Angel's voice said through the walkie-talkie.

Specter approached and pet Phantom's back. "I think everyone is okay, but they definitely had some kind of crazy encounter. They just kept on walking and their faces said nothing but double zero. It was really creepy and—Oh God! I forgot Mr. Crussman and that waitress!"

Roger Crussman had past the woods. He was closing in on Raven River's cold dark tomb. Wanda the waitress was less than ten feet behind him. Their blank faces hadn't changed as they headed towards the river. Roger Crussman's feet splashed. The wet icy sensation raced up his body. He kept walking anyway. Soon, Raven River was up to his ankles then past his knees. Wanda the waitress followed. Her foot was ready to step into the water, when Specter charged out of the woods, spun her around, and slapped her on the cheek. Wanda, like the others before her, blinked and held the side of her blushed face.

"Whad you do that for?" she said, then looked around. "How did I get here?"

Specter didn't answer. She stepped past Wanda and took out her magic whip. Roger Crussman was waist high in Raven River. Specter snapped her whip and the wampum cord wrapped around his torso. Specter pulled with all her might, nudging Mr. Crussman back to shore. It took Wanda a few seconds to realize that something had gone wrong at some point in the evening. She helped Specter pull Roger Crussman back to the shore. Specter gave the slap. Roger looked around, frowning.

"Who are you?" he said. "Are you one of them Monster Cops? Where am I? Awww, my feet are wet! I hate Halloween."

"Take a number," Specter said to herself and rested her back on a nearby tree.

CHAPTER
32

When Angel *Roller Blade* to *Donnelly's Bar and Grill*, she didn't notice anything unusual at first. From afar, it looked almost peaceful. There were no broken windows, no signs of fighting, and no blood on the walls. She took out her bow anyway and skated up to the restaurant/pub. She opened one of the glass doors.

The lights were still on. The grill was sizzling black hamburgers. There were dirty glasses and dishes on some of the tables, but there were no persons enjoying their dinner or engaging in conversation. If Donnelly wanted to close early, he did a lousy job shutting the place down. Angel took hold of her walkie-talkie and pushed the "talk" button.

"Jadeite, you might wanna stay alert," she said. "I'm in *Donnelly's Bar and Grill* right now. There's no one in sight, not even Donnelly himself. I'm gonna take a look around, check the register, the kitchen, b-b-bah. If I don't find anything, you better get on the phone to the police. This may be human-related. Over."

"No problem," Jadeite's voice said through the walkie. "Just be careful."

"I will," Angel said. "Out."

Angel reached behind her back and took out a silver-tipped arrow from her quiver. She lined it with the cord on her bow. She pulled the arrow back, ready for anything that could possibly attack her. She skated into the bar and grill's core. The place was too quiet and too empty for her comfort. She glanced around at the unoccupied tables and booths and noticed that many of the coat racks next to them were being used. Coats of all sizes and colors hung like tiny drapes. There were also pocketbooks left on some of the chairs.

I think we can rule out robbery, Angel thought. What happened here, a fire drill?

There was the muffled sound of breaking glass.

Angel yelped and pointed her arrow towards the bar.

The swinging doors next to the bar, which lead to the kitchen, pushed open. Jack padded out with a bottle of rum in his scorched green hand. He glared at Angel.

"More," he said. "More voodoo rum."

"Try college," Angel said. "I did."

Jack's suit and top hat looked too authentic to be a costume, unless someone went to an antique store and was willing to spend a fortune. Part of that fortune would have to go for the make-up job on his face. Angel aimed her silver arrow at him.

"Put the bottle down," she said.

Jack smashed it on the tile floor.

"Close enough," Angel said. "Now put your hands on the wall."

"If I did that," he said in his grated voice, "I might drop my lantern!"

He raised the glowing blue lantern for her to see. Its illumination and hypnotic effect hit her almost instantly. Angel felt her joints freeze up. Though she tried to look away, she couldn't. She fired the arrow with her last shred of willpower.

The silver broadhead zipped through the thick air between them. It hit Jack in the arm that held his lantern. He wailed and dropped the lantern to the floor. It made an empty metallic thud as it hit. With the horrible light out of her eyes, Angel snapped her mind and body back to reality and skated out of the bar and grill. When she got outside, she reached for her walkie-talkie.

"Angel to Jadeite," she said into the receiver, "I'm gonna need backup! We've got a situation here! Over!"

"I'll be right there. Out!" Jadeite's said through the walkie.

Angel took out her white squirt gun filled with holy water. Jack came out of *Donnelly's Bar and Grill*. The lantern was back in his hand. He was about twenty feet away from her when he pulled out the silver arrow from his bicep and tossed it aside.

"That wasn't nice," he said. "If you hadn't done that, I might have let ya live."

He raised his lantern and walked towards her.

Angel shut her eyes and took a few steps back. She pulled the trigger. Holy water jet out. Most of the shots missed. The few that hit Jack, made him wince, but not enough to stop him from closing in on her. To Jack, they were like bee stings.

"I hope you know how to swim, my dear!"

Jack's already huge eyes widened as he heard a loud "snap." A string of wampum wrapped itself around his lantern like a snake. He turned to his right and saw Moonbeam and Specter, who had her magic whip coiled around his biggest asset. Specter yanked her whip. The lantern flew out of Jack's hand. It landed on the street, but didn't break.

Angel opened her eyes just in time to see what happened. "Don't look into the lantern!" she said.

"I don't need my lantern to take care of you kiddies," Jack said. "I think it'll be more fun to strangle the life out of you and then bite your heads off, one by one!"

Jack intended to make good on his promise as he charged for Angel. When he got close enough, she squirted him in the eyes with holy water and gave him an uppercut. Jack howled as he held his face. He was still on his feet though. When he put his green hands down, traces of maroon blood dripped out of his orange eyes. He growled at Angel and seized her throat.

Specter snapped her wampum whip again. The cord wrapped around one of Jack's legs. Jack threw Angel onto the ground, grabbed one end of the whip, and pulled Specter towards him, much the way Specter snatched the lantern out of his hand. He grabbed Specter by the neck with one hand, her thigh with the other hand, and lifted her above his head.

Jack took a second or two to decide where to throw Specter. Thoughts flashed through his mind. He could toss her on top of the girl dressed in black and white or he could throw her through *Donnelly's* glass door or fling her into the street. Maybe a car would hit her. That would be convenient. He realized his thoughts and visualizations took too long when Moonbeam jabbed his back with the end of a silver staff. The jab caused a sharp ball of pain in Jack's spine. His grip on Specter loosened. She fell to the ground. When Jack turned around, the tip of Moonbeam's staff smacked him across the face. He stumbled back.

"Your lantern ain't gonna work on me," Moonbeam said. "We've got you outnumbered. Do yourself a favor and surrender."

"Take your best shot, lad!" Jack said.

Moonbeam twirled his staff and swung with all his might.

Jack caught it and kicked his opponent in the stomach. Before Moonbeam's knees could hit the ground, Jack circled behind him. His powerful arms wrapped around Moonbeam's neck. Jack faced Angel and Specter. Moonbeam tried to struggle free.

"One move and I twist his head off!" he said.

Specter froze, her whip drawn back.

Angel had another silver arrow aimed at him. "What do you want?"

"I want to go back into the bar and continue my business," Jack said. "Leave me be with my voodoo rum and I'll let your friend go."

"Assaulting a Pniese is a hundred years in Poltergeist Prison," Angel said. "You assaulted three. If you let go of our friend and cooperate with us, maybe you'll be released in only two-hundred years."

"Cooperate?" Jack said, "Be imprisoned? No one is going imprison me ever again! Go ahead! Try to shoot me. I'm willing to bet that I can break this boy's neck before your arrow can reach my face!"

"My arrow isn't the only weapon aimed at you," Angel said.

"What?" Jack said.

He planned to ask what Angel meant by her remark when he felt a horrible burning hit the back of his head. It was painful enough for him to loosen his grip and clutch the back of his skull. That was all the distraction Moonbeam needed to roll away.

When Jack turned around, he saw Jadeite. One of Jadeite's green combat boots was on the street, the other on top of his skateboard. A slingshot was in his hand. The elastic part of it was stretched back, nearly grinding his big chin. In the slingshot's leather cradle was a wax ball that contained garlic and wolfsbane.

Jack knew he was outnumbered and did the only thing he could think of. He dove for his lantern and sprinted away. Angel fired her arrow. It hit *Donnelly's* front brick wall as Jack sped around the corner.

"Get him!" Specter said. She and Jadeite raced after Jack. When they ran around the corner, their adversary was gone. Only a dark alley with a hint of fog inches above the street. There were no dumpsters or sewer covers for Jack to hide in. He was nearby no doubt, but far enough away to know that they wouldn't catch him.

"I don't get it," Jadeite said. "My pellets should have knocked him to the ground."

"Yes, I know," Specter said. "I'm not sure who or what that was."

"Well he's definitely no vampire or zombie," Angel said, as she and Moonbeam caught up with their allies. "My silver arrows and holy water didn't do a whole lot of damage to him either. It barely slowed him down, actually. This guy is definitely in a class all by himself."

"So what do we do?" Moonbeam said.

"We gotta find out who this guy is," Angel said. "Once we can classify him, we'll know how to hurt him and more importantly, how to stop him."

CHAPTER 33

"Let me do it," Twilight said.

"Will you back off?" Colt said.

They were in the rear of Saint Roland's cathedral. Twilight had told Colt to get his grapple and cable ready. Since the church was locked up, they had to scale up the wall to the balcony roof. When Colt asked why, Twilight stated that he had allies up there who liked to play cards. The trouble came when Colt tried to throw his grapple and get it to lock behind the balcony's guardrail. Twilight accomplished it on his first try, but Colt failed after four attempts.

"You gotta aim with your eyes and put some muscle into it," Twilight said.

"I know, thank you," Colt said, slightly annoyed.

He swung the grapple around in a circle. When he felt there was enough speed generating, he threw the steel cable in the air. The grapple hook sailed upward. It tapped the guardrail and dropped back down.

"Heads up!" Colt said.

They bolted out of the way just in time to see the grapple hook clank against the concrete driveway and bounce once.

Twilight groaned. "You didn't practice enough."

"Oh, don't go there," Colt picked up his hook. "I practiced plenty. I probably would've gotten it by now if you weren't nagging me and looking over my shoulder like a freakin' vulture."

"Fine," Twilight said. He took a step back with his palms held up, "I won't say a word."

Colt took hold of his grapple hook again and spun it. He focused on the guardrail on the church's roof and took a deep breath. With a great heave, the hook jumped up the building and tangled into the guardrail.

"Yeah!" Colt said, "See? No nagging and I do just fine. Maybe now you'll give me some space and a little credit."

Twilight stepped forward and tugged his cable. "Not bad. Not good either. My 'nagging,' as you put it, is for a reason. There may be a situation where you may have to do this with all kinds of distractions around you. You gotta do it right and do it right the first time."

Twilight climbed up the church wall. Colt fell silent for a second or two. He knew that Twilight had a valid point, but then returned to his sarcastic persona.

"Well excuuuuuuuuuuuse me!" And started to climb up his rope.

When Colt reached the top, he saw four gargoyles sitting around a card table playing poker. They were all blue-skinned with lemon yellow eyes, button-like noses, folded up bat wings on their backs, and horns just above their pointed ears. Two of them wore gold loop earrings. One had a nose ring. They were loud and obnoxious as one of them yelled out with sharp teeth, "Full house!" The other gargoyles groaned and slapped their hands on the table to start over.

Colt jumped over the guardrail and took out his squirt gun.

Twilight slapped his hand. "What're you doing?"

The gargoyles noticed Colt's action as well.

"Take it easy, kid!"

"We ain't done nothin'!"

The reaction confused Colt. He turned to Twilight. "They're legit?"

"Of course we're legit!" the gargoyle with the nose ring said. "Why do we always get bum raps? We were created to watch over and protect. Why else would they have stone carvings of us on top of churches?"

"Sorry," Colt said. "I guess the air up here is a little thinner and it messed with my head."

"Boys, this is my Colt," Twilight said. "Colt, this is Rufus, Tokey, Arullus, and Howie."

Colt gave a surprised look after the last name. "Howie?"

"Please," Howie the gargoyle said, "no 'Deal or No Deal' jokes."

"What brings you by, Twilight?" Arullus the nose-ringed gargoyle said as he collected the playing cards while the others pushed a portion of their playing chips to Tokey, who had the full house.

"I need you guys to keep your eyes peeled," Twilight said. "There's been a robbery and it was done by two teens. One of them is dressed like a ninja, the other has his face done up like a dead man."

"Sure ting," Howie the gargoyle said. "One more hand and we'll take a look 'round town, see what's goin' down."

"Thanks, boys," Twilight said, then turned to Colt. "Let's get going."

"But I just got up here," Colt said.

"Let's go."

"Ain't there a quicker way down?"

"Sure, kid," Rufus said. "You can get to the ground twice as fast—just don't use the rope!"

The laughter that came out of the ghastly gamblers reminded Colt of his father's friends when they came to the house every *Super Bowl* Sunday, carrying an eight foot sub on their shoulders and smoking nasty-smelling cigars.

"Hi ya doin' Marvin?"

"Don't worry Shayla! We ain't gonna stain no carpet this time around!"

"Pass me a cold one!"

"LET'S GO, *PATS*!"

All such comments were made as they donned their *Patriots* jerseys (or whatever team they were routing for) and gazed at the big-screen TV in masculine bliss. It almost made Colt chuckle, because under different circumstances, the gargoyles and his father's friends probably would have got along.

Twilight and Colt lowered themselves to the ground. They coiled up their grappling hooks and cables and stuck them in their proper place on the back of their belts. Their walkie-talkies spoke as they sauntered towards their '57 Chevy in the cathedral's parking lot.

"Twilight, Colt, come in! Over!" It was Angel's voice.

They picked up their walkies and spoke at the same time. "Go ahead."

They glanced at each other.

"I'll do the talking," Twilight said.

"Whatever," Colt said. "I'll go make myself useful. Maybe wash the car."

Ignoring Colt, Twilight said, "Go ahead. Over."

"We just had an encounter with a entity of unknown origin. Over," Angel said through the walkie-talkie.

"An unknown entity?" Twilight said, "I don't understand. Was it a ghoul or some kind of ghost? Over."

"I don't think so," Angel said. "This guy was powerful. Our weapons only slowed him down. He might be some kind of demon, but I can't imagine what kind. Over."

Twilight jogged over to the car where Colt stood, his back against the passenger side window.

"Open the door and unlock the glove compartment," Twilight said.

Colt obeyed. When the glove compartment was opened, he discovered that like the rest of the car, it too had been modified. Instead of any empty space, there was a mini computer screen and a keyboard on the inside compartment door. The computer screen had the following displayed:

WELCOME PNIESE

MENU

1 - map of Sleepy Owl and surrounding towns

2 – files of known supernatural criminals

3 – Mythology index

4 – creature identification

5 – files on known supernatural allies

6 – Pniese history

7 – other

"Okay," Twilight said to his walkie-talkie. "We'll look it up. Over."

Twilight kneeled down next to Colt and pushed "4."

"Yo, just take care of the CB," Colt said. "I can do this, aaaright?"

"Fair enough," Twilight said and turned his attention back to his walkie-talkie. "What can you tell us about this guy? Over."

"He was about five feet-ten," Angel said, "and weighed about…I'd say…no more than 130 pounds."

Colt typed the information into the car's computer.

"He had green skin and this long horrible orange hair and orange eyes," Angel said.

"Go on," Twilight said. "Was he dressed in anything unusual? Over."

"Yeah, this dusty ol' suit with a top hat and coat tails," Angel said. "He also had this lantern with him and I think it must have some kind of evil magic because it nearly paralyzed me and several others. All he kept saying was 'I want my voodoo rum,' whatever that is. Over."

"You getting all this?" Twilight said.

"Yeah," Colt said. "What do I do now?"

"Press 'enter.'"

Colt hit the key.

Twilight kneeled next to Colt once again and watched as the computer made a search of all the available information on their colleagues' attacker. The results came up a few seconds later.

"Aw man," Twilight said.

"We still there?" Angel said through the walkie-talkie, "What have we got? Over."

"Trouble," Twilight said. "You're right. This guy's in a class all by himself. You might want to swing by Saint Roland's cathedral and see what I'm talking about. Over."

"We'll be right there," Angel said. "Over and out."

CHAPTER 34

Jadeite had the slowest form of transportation. Although he was an expert with the skateboard, it took him the longer to arrive at Saint Roland's cathedral parking lot than Angel who had *Roller Blades* as well as Moonbeam and Specter, who rode on Phantom.

Before he arrived, Jadeite went back to the town square where he met Count Torlock under Angel's orders. Count Torlock looked like a gallant gentleman of the nineteenth century in his traditional *Dracula* outfit, long sideburns, and white skin. Of course, it was a secret that Count Torlock was both an actual vampire and a Pniese ally. He was dancing with Darla McConnell, who worked at the local post office while Spider Web, the macabre rock band, played the *Electric Slide*. Darla was dressed as a giant butterfly in a tight yellow body suit and wings made of nylon and twine. A yellow glitter mask covered her upper face as she smiled at her dance partner.

Jadeite held his skateboard under his arm and tapped Count Torlock's shoulder.

The Count turned and nodded. "Jadeite! Happy Halloween! I'm sorry, but you can't cut in. I'm having far too much fun dancing with this elegant young lady."

Darla's cheeks blushed. She giggled.

"Duty calls, Torlock," Jadeite whispered in his ear.

The Count's grin faded. He bowed to his butterfly dancer. "I apologize, my dear. There is something I must take care of, but do stay in the area. I shall return for you."

"Okay, Count," Darla said. "Don't take too long."

Count Torlock followed Jadeite to the town square party's outskirts, where they could get more privacy. When Jadeite felt the coast was clear he said, "I need you to keep an eye on things for a little while."

"Certainly," the Count said, "how long?"

"Maybe a half-hour, give or take," Jadeite said. "We've run into a little problem and a huddle has been called."

"Nothing too serious, I hope." Torlock said.

"Nah," Jadeite said. "Well, nothing we can't handle. Contact us if anything gets too out of hand."

"Don't worry," Torlock said. "Go to your meeting."

"Thanks, dude."

They shook hands and went their separate ways. Torlock returned to his vibrant dance partner and Jadeite went towards Saint Roland's cathedral. Jadeite put down his skateboard and his foot started rowing to build up speed. He glanced back to take a final look at the party.

Then turned around and came upon a hideous face with snakes for hair.

He gasped and nearly stumbled off his skateboard.

Two gorgons were in front of him. They both had iguana green skin and were dressed in light blue togas. Their snake hairs slithered about, flicking their tongues at Jadeite. The legend of the gorgons is that they have the power to turn persons into stone with one look in their eyes. This was true. When their species started to make appearances in Sleepy Owl in the early twentieth century, the Pniese passed a law: gorgons wear sunglasses at all times. In the case of Herebus and his wife, Ariel, no laws had been broken.

"Jadeite!" Ariel said, "Thank the Gods!"

"Hi, is anything wrong?"

"Indeed, there is," Herebus said. "Our daughter, Pandusa, is missing."

"When was the last time you saw her?"

"About an hour ago," Herebus said. "We've been looking for the last forty-five minutes, but we just can't find her. She usually stays within the town square."

"Please help us find our baby!" Ariel said. She put her hands on Jadeite's wide shoulders, "We don't want to leave her behind when curfew takes effect."

"It's all right," Jadeite said. "I'll send word out. I'm sure she'll turn up way before curfew."

"I'm afraid the situation is worse than you think," Herebus said. He reached into his toga and pulled out a pair of pink, cat's eye sunglasses. "This is all we've found so far."

Jadeite groaned. "Dude, tell me those aren't hers."

"I wish I could," Herebus said.

"Okay," Jadeite took the sunglasses. "I'll see what I can do."

Halloween night has never been easy. Last year, they dealt with an insane entity called Bloody Mary and the year before that, an undead circus. Now they have to deal with a missing gorgon who has no sunglasses on, which means anyone that crosses her path is going to turn to stone. Then, of course, there's the psychotic being with the lantern that seems to be invincible.

CHAPTER 35

All the Pniese gathered around the mini computer screen in the '57 Chevy's glove compartment to witness the results that the digital filing system had come up with.

"His name is Jack," Twilight read from the screen. "In life, he was a volatile man who drank himself to death. Because of his cruelty, he was forbidden to enter Heaven's gates. The Devil found him and decided to personally escort him into Hell. On the way, Jack noticed an apple tree and asked the Devil if he could have an apple before they continue their journey. The Devil agreed, but when he climbed up the tree to get some, Jack took out a knife and carved a cross on the bark. The Devil was trapped in the tree. Jack told him that he would get rid of the cross if the Devil would let him go. The Devil agreed and Jack was free once more."

"Well, that would explain why he's on the loose," Angel said.

"Wait, it gets so much better," Twilight said. "According to legend, Jack lived long enough for two lifetimes and became bored. He went to the gates of the Devil's Domain, hoping to find a place of acceptance, but the Devil refused to let him in. Jack told the Devil that he has to be let in because it's far too dark to return to the mortal world. This was Jack's mistake. The Devil took a lump of coal and threw it at Jack. When Jack caught the coal, it scorched his hand and changed him into the hideous thing you guys battled earlier."

"What about the lantern?" Specter said.

"The lantern was also given to him by the Devil," Twilight said. "It had other pieces of coal in it as well as the power to hypnotize his victims. However, the piece of coal that Jack caught seems to be the key. It acted like a bind and forced him to walk the earth for all eternity. This is where the term, 'Jack o' lantern' came from."

"Whoa, whoa, I'm confused about something," Colt said. "If this guy is doomed to walk the earth for all eternity, then how come he was spotted in *Donnelly's Bar and Grill*? Shouldn't he just be passing through?"

"Technically, yes," Twilight said. "Jack hates people and wants nothing more than to indulge in drinking. He's only allowed to stop walking for a minute or two, which means he shouldn't have been in *Donnelly's* as long as you guys said he was."

"Maybe the computer made a mistake," Colt said.

"Or maybe he's not forced to walk the earth anymore," Moonbeam said. "What if that piece of coal burned itself out after hundreds of years?"

"He's got a point," Angel said. "What does it say about stopping him?"

Twilight read a few more lines and frowned. "There doesn't seem to be a way. Our weapons will slow him down, but as far as containing him? There's no information on the matter. Basically, Jack is holding all the cards. If Moonbeam is right and that piece of coal kept him bound for all that time and it's no longer burning, then Jack may very well be free to do whatever he wants, whenever he wants."

A hush fell over the Pniese. Colt read the computer file again. "That ain't right. There's got to be some catch. What if we get another piece of coal and have some witches or wizards use their magic? Wouldn't that force Jack back to his long walk?"

"No can do," Twilight said. "Witch and wizard magic only works temporarily in this world. In another few weeks, Jack would be free again."

"Can't we just put him in Poltergeist Prison?" Jadeite said.

"The guards wouldn't take him," Twilight said. "All inmates of Poltergeist Prison have to be supernatural. No human or miscellaneous beings permitted. According to the computer, Jack isn't supernatural. He's cursed and that's not the same thing."

"That's it," Angel said.

Everyone turned to her, flabbergasted.

"I know how to stop him," she said. "Just find him and keep him busy."

"How?" Jadeite said.

"You'll find a way," Angel said. "I'll be back."

She started to skate away and almost got to the end of Saint Roland's parking lot when she heard Jadeite call out for her to wait. She spun around. "What is it?"

"We got another problem," he said. "There's a gorgon missing and she's got no sunglasses on. How do you wanna handle that?"

Angel covered her eyes. "You got to be kidding," she muttered. "How are we suppose to find someone that can turn you into stone if you look for her?"

They paused in thought for some time, repeating the situation over in their minds. Pandusa, the missing gorgon, would be easy to track down. All one had to do was follow the stone figures and eventually, you would find her, but then what? One look, accidental or not, and you would be a statue. The answer hit Jadeite and Angel at the same time.

"Marty!" they said and pointed at each other.

"Go fill them in," Angel said. "Time's wasting."

She darted away on her *Roller Blades* when Jadeite called out to her again. "Where are you going!"

"To collect on a favor!" she said without turning around.

CHAPTER 36

The teen dressed like a ninja took a close look at one of the gold coins he and his friend had taken. It was nighttime, but the coin, like the other ninety-nine in the crock, was polished so well that it glowed like dull sunshine.

"There's no way this's real," he said. "No one would be stupid enough to carry a pot of real gold."

"Shut up, Daryl," the painted-face kid said. "I'm telling ya, that ain't no chocolate wrapper or paint. I think we took the real thing."

The boys were sitting at a picnic table next to the Trevor Wallace Memorial Field where the Sleepy Owl Tomahawks played baseball. To their left was the children's playground and to their right was the Sleepy Owl football field. The ninja pulled off his hood, revealing a freckled face and thick red hair. If Willy Hynes were in the area, he would recognize him as Daryl Julson. The other teen in face paint was Bobby McHooley, a friend of Daryl's, but not necessarily a friend of Willy's.

Bobby loved to get into trouble. Although it was late October, he already had five detentions under his belt. Most of his school crimes came from picking on Ike Buchanen, the class nerd. Bobby often smacked books out of Ike's hand or try to stick a piece of masking tape saying, "kick me hard!" on his back. Sometimes Bobby got away with it and Ike would walk around as long as an hour, before a teacher or a sympathetic student discovered the cruel note. Bobby loved to pick on those smaller than him, and Daryl, being three inches shorter and much skinnier, decided years ago to get in good with Bobby or he might be a potential victim as well. When Bobby told him to wear something dark and stealthy on Halloween, Daryl didn't hesitate to get his hood from an old ninja costume. And when a leprechaun came hobbling along earlier in the evening, dragging his crock of gold, and scouring for a good hiding spot, Bobby couldn't resist and took out his can of shaving cream.

"Maybe we should give it back," Daryl said. "That guy could be talking to the police right now."

"I ain't afraid," Bobby said, taking a coin from the crock. "Are you?"

Daryl didn't answer right away. He looked around at the surrounding parks and saw no one in sight. "No, not really. I mean, what's that guy gonna do? Go up to an officer dressed like a leprechaun and say 'they stole me crock of gold'?"

"Now you're making sense," Bobby said. "Tomorrow, I'm going to go to *Don's* jewelry store and see if these coins are legit. If they are, do you know how much they'd be worth?"

Daryl looked into the crock. "Hundreds, maybe even thousands. I could get an iPhone with that kind of money."

"An iPhone?" Bobby said, "You could get your own apartment with that kind of money. Imagine it: the only thirteen-year-olds with a place of their own. Do you know how cool that would be? My big brother doesn't even have a place of his own and he's twice my age—friggin' loser."

"My own place," Daryl repeated the idea in his mind like he was watching the best part of a movie. "That would be cool. I could put whatever I wanted in there. No stupid flower wallpaper or doilies like my Mom has."

"Yeah, we could put our own stuff in there," Bobby said. "Like posters and colored light bulbs instead of the regular kind."

"Hey, what will we tell the police if they do find out?" Daryl said.

"We'll tell 'em that we found it in some bushes," Bobby said. "Remember, we were in disguise when we took it from that midget, so there's no way they can identify us. Trust me, bud, we got it made. They got nothing on us. All we gotta do is just lay low until the heat dies down."

Bobby's father loved to watch Mafia movies and every now and again, Daryl noticed that Bobby would utter such cliché lines as "they got nothing on us" and "laying low until the heat dies down."

The idea of his own place stirred in Bobby's mind to the point where he was psyched of the possibility. He tilted the pot and let some of the coins fall on the picnic table. It was time to split their profits right down the middle—unless of course, Bobby could figure out a way to manipulate the count so he got more than Daryl did. Daryl's attention seemed to be elsewhere as he looked behind Bobby and gazed with fascination. Bobby took notice after counting out fifteen coins.

"What is it?"

Daryl didn't respond. He just stared, void of any emotion.

Bobby turned around and saw a light blue orb nodding in the distance.

The orb was coming closer. A dark figure followed behind.

Bobby ran his palm across the picnic table, forcing the coins he spilled to tumble back into the crock. He got up from his seat and turned to the figure and orb that was drawing nearer.

"Who is that?" Bobby said, "What are you doing here?"

As the orb approached, Bobby got a better look at the figure. It was a disgusting-looking man with green skin, orange wisps of hair, and a crooked smile.

"I want voodoo rum."

"What's that?" Bobby said, "Hey what's with that light of yours? Is it battery- operated?"

"Show me where to get voodoo rum," Jack said.

Although Bobby was big for his age—five feet, five inches and growing, Jack was bigger. Jack's appearance was also more terrifying than Bobby's face paint could ever be. Bobby's make-up started to chip off a long time ago and much of the white paint had smeared on his black sweatshirt collar. For some reason, Jack's "make-up" didn't smear or chip. That made Bobby wonder. Still, he tried to sound as tough as he could.

"Look, man," he said, "I don't know nothing about voodoo rum."

"Then you're of no use to me," Jack said. He held up his lantern to Bobby's eyes and watched the young man's pupils contract and fall under his power. Within seconds, Bobby was as paralyzed as Daryl was.

Jack lowered his lantern. "Walk to the nearest body of water and don't stop."

Bobby's subconscious mind begged him to run to the nearest police officer, but Jack's influence proved too strong. Bobby walked towards Raven River, leaving behind his share of the gold.

Jack approached Daryl. "You will lead me to voodoo rum, won't you, lad?"

Daryl managed to nod.

"Goooood," Jack stretched his reply. "Show me."

Daryl was able to move his body. Like all of Jack's victims, his subconscious mind wanted him to scream for help. Instead, Daryl's sneakers moved one foot in front of the other. He walked to the nearest place he could think of that would satisfy his new master. He never heard of voodoo rum, but assumed that it was the same as regular rum. The police station was less than fifteen minutes away if he headed south, but he couldn't move in that direction. He had his orders. He headed in the opposite direction towards a convenience store about a mile away.

CHAPTER
37

Angel had taken off her *Roller Blades*, tied the laces together, and hung them around her neck. White combat boots had been stepped into because it was too difficult to skate through the woods. Her miniature flashlight was the only source of light in the forest primeval that occupied eastern Sleepy Owl. The trees' bark patterns themselves seem to make malign faces at her when the light exposed them. Dead leaves and branches crunched under her feet. The sound of chirping bats was heard above. It was intimidating to be there alone and though she had her holy water pistol in her other white-gloved hand, she would have felt better if she were holding her bow. Unfortunately, because of the dark atmosphere and the stretching branches and vines, her bow would likely get tangled more easily than a squirt gun would.

Where is it? she said to herself, come on, where is it?

The sound of Raven River licking the shores with its cold silver water was in the distance. It mixed with the bat squeals, leaf shuffling, and branch snapping. A far off police siren bellowed. Finding Raven River was the easy part. The difficulty was being in the right place in the forest.

She turned northeast and drew closer to Raven River. The ground became softer. She saw slashed openings of gray light between the somber tree trunks. As she sauntered closer to her goal, something pinched her leg.

She gasped and looked down, flashlight first.

Her pant leg caught on the jagged branch of a fallen oak. Angel breathed a sigh of relief, tucked her squirt gun into her belt, and yanked the cotton material off of the sharp wooden point. A light tear was heard and a hole was made, but she didn't care. She had something important to find. She found it a few yards ahead.

She hurried over to the boundary between the forest and Raven River. A large rib bone hung from a tree branch by a thin rope. The rib bone had several punctures in it, including horizontally long oval-shaped ones at each end. Angel had no idea where it came from or who hung it on the branch. She only knew three things: her predecessor and cousin, Megan Daniels, showed it to her when she was a Colt, the rib bone probably didn't come from anything human, and it most likely wouldn't be found on any other night besides Halloween.

She unhooked it from the tree branch. "Well…here goes."

Angel took a breath and blew into the rib bone. A low musical moan came out of the other end. It sounded like a man being tortured whose screams were muffled because his lips had been glued together.

Angel put the rib bone back…and waited.

She saw the fog form and swirl above the river, creating a mystical wall. She reached into her pocket and took out three Mercury head dimes. They weren't worth much in this world, but unlike today's dimes, they were silver and that was all she needed. The fog grew thicker. In the far-off light rapids, a tall figure made its way to shore. Whoever it was held an oar and took its time paddling. Its dark robe and hood covered its identity. The boat it was standing on appeared as rickety as an ice puddle in April and as old as the moon that shined on it. It hit the shore with a hard thud, inches from Angel.

The tall ferryman raised its hood. The first things Angel saw were its glowing blue eyes. It was a man with Native American facial features, much like the ferryman in Willy Hynes's dream, yet somehow darker and less human. Angel could make out long straight hair through the inside hood's blackness. The ferryman stuck out his wrinkled hand. He unfolded talon fingers.

"Three silver pieces," his voice was base low, but clear.

Angel placed the dimes into the ferryman's scarred palm. He backed up enough for her to climb into the boat. She sat down.

"Poltergeist Prison," she said.

The ferryman nodded and turned around. This made Angel feel more at ease as she no longer needed to look into the dark hood with eyes as bright as natural gas from her kitchen stove. The boat coughed away from the shore and floated towards deeper Raven River. It was just the two of them for miles around, but if one had been watching, they would have seen the boat and its passengers drift into the fog and vanish.

"It's Mr. Coogan from the barber shop," Moonbeam said as he felt the stone face with his bare hand.

"At least we're on the right track," Specter said.

They were on Littlefield Drive where Mr. Coogan lived. Mr. Coogan was now frozen in a slow walking position, his right foot in front. His left heel came off the ground. A plastic bag full of candy lay by his feet. He looked shocked. His mouth was wide open and eyebrows were raised. His head was tilted to the left and faced the woods, which lead Moonbeam and Specter to believe that a gorgon, probably Pandusa, had taken him by surprise on his way home from the nearby general store.

"We should lay him down by the weeds," Specter said. "That way, he won't attract much attention."

"All right," Moonbeam said and felt for Mr. Coogan's solid chest.

"Once the gorgons leave our world, he should return to normal," Specter said, "Give him a push…but carefully."

Moonbeam obliged. Just as Mr. Coogan was going off balance and started to fall, Specter caught his heavy head and laid him down on the grass. Suddenly, Moonbeam heard the sound of talking adults and laughing children.

"Heads up, trick-or-treaters."

Specter rose to her feet and joined Moonbeam in front of Mr. Coogan's exposed foot souls, trying to cover them up. Two adults came into view. Specter recognized them right away as Mr. and Mrs. Dayers and their children, Manny, Tim, and Lisa. Mr. Dayers was not wearing a costume, though he looked as if he were dressed like a lumberjack with his full beard and flannel-checkered shirt. Mrs. Dayers was also void of costume, donned in a thick coat and gloves. Their children carried neon green and orange glow sticks. Their pillowcases were teemed with candy, apples, and gum. Manny, the oldest at eight, was dressed as

Harry Potter. Tim, the middle child at six, was *Pikachu* from *Pokemon* and Lisa, the youngest at five, was a princess. She skipped in her pink tutu and glitter crown. The Dayers family probably would have ignored Moonbeam and Specter and their attempts to conceal Mr. Coogan, but there was one problem. Phantom, the beautiful white stallion, was next to them and the Dayers children were animal lovers.

"Oh wow!" Tim said as he ran up to the supernatural horse.

Manny looked at Specter. "Is he yours? Where did you get him?"

"Actually," Specter said, looking nervous and pointing at Moonbeam. "It's his."

"Where did you get him?" Manny said, this time to Moonbeam.

"Well, he was…" Moonbeam gulped, "kind of a present. From my relatives."

"You're wicked lucky," Manny said, then turned to his parents. "Can we get a horse like this one?"

"Where are we going to keep it?" Mr. Dayers said.

"My room!" Tim stepped in.

"I don't think so," Mrs. Dayers said. "We already got a dog and a cat and a bunch of fish and you always forget to feed them."

"Aw mom," Manny said, "I would take care of this one—honest."

Specter noticed that Phantom had lowered his head enough for Lisa Dayers to pet him and give him a kiss. "What's his name?"

"Phantom," Specter said.

"What kind of name is that?" Tim said.

"A phantom is like a ghost, Tim," Mr. Dayers said. "They probably call him that because he's all white like a ghost. Am I right?"

Specter touched her nose. "Bingo."

"All right kids," Mrs. Dayers said, "say 'good-bye' to Phantom and this nice young man and woman. We still have plenty more houses to go."

The Dayers family bid farewell to Moonbeam and Specter. They gave Phantom one last pat between the eyes before they resumed their yearly candy collecting. The Monster Cops waited until they were out of range before sighing with relief.

"It would have been fun to explain the statue of Mr. Coogan, don't you think?" Moonbeam said.

"A blast," Specter said. "We've got another problem though."

"What?"

"Me," Specter said. "You're immune to turning to stone because of your blindness, but if I find Pandusa, it's not going to do any good because I'll end up like Mr. Coogan."

"You got a point," Moonbeam said. "Well, I can't do this myself and Phantom won't be much help in telling me if we run…across…"

Moonbeam began to brainstorm. Specter noticed.

"Phantom," he muttered and felt for the horse's soft thin hair. Phantom emit a faint whinny.

"What? What about Phantom?"

"He's immune to turning into stone, right?"

"Yes, he's classifies as a ghost officially," Specter said. "So?"

"So?" Moonbeam said, "So, what do they call you?"

"What are talking about?" Specter said, "You know what—hey. It just might work."

She took out her wampum whip from the side of her belt. With one end in each hand, she started to use the whip as a jump rope and became more transparent with every skip she made.

"You realize if any people see me, there's going to be trouble, right?" she said.

"It's the risk we're going to have to take," Moonbeam said. He mounted onto Phantom. "Something tells me that if Mr. Coogan saw Pandusa, then others must have too."

CHAPTER 39

"There it is," Colt said. He pointed at the picnic table.

The '57 Chevy pulled into the parking lot next to Trevor Wallace Memorial Field. Twilight drove the car under a parking light and cut the engine. They received a tip from some trick-or-treaters that a ninja and a boy with his face painted like a skull were seen less than a half-hour ago at the picnic tables. They were believed to be counting and trading candy. Twilight and Colt got out of the car. They sauntered up to the picnic table that had a black pot on top of it. When they were close enough, they saw the gold inside the crock and a few coins on the table.

Twilight examined one of the coins. "This is definitely Darby's gold."

"Great," Colt said. "Case closed."

"Wrong."

"What do you mean?"

"We found the gold, but not the thieves."

"Whoa, hold the phone," said Colt. "According to you and the man from *Oz*, the thieves were human. I thought we weren't suppose to deal with people."

"That's not what concerns me," Twilight said. He tossed the coin in his hand into the pot, "I'm wondering why the thieves didn't take their payday with them."

"You think something happened to them?" Colt said.

Twilight nodded.

"Maybe Darby hired the *Lollipop Kids* to beat 'em up." This made Colt snicker through his nose. He looked to his mentor to share the mirth. Twilight didn't. "You know, the '*Lollipop Kids*?'"

Colt weakly sang out of one side of his mouth. "We represent the Lollipop Kids, the Lolly…pop…kids…"

Twilight folded his arms.

"Oh, it's okay for you to sing '*Rubber Duckie*,'" said Colt, "but I hum the *Munchkin land* theme and you're aggravated. Go figure."

"This could be serious," Twilight said. "We gotta find those kids now and make sure they're okay."

"They probably thought the gold was fake and decided to go egg a few houses," Colt said. "You gotta admit, the gold does look a little too shiny and cartoony to be real. I definitely wouldn't believe it was real anyway."

"I hope you're right," Twilight said. He took out his walkie-talkie and pressed the "talk" button. "Attention everyone, we found Darby's gold, but there's no sign of the perpetrators, leaving suspicion that supernaturals may have taken matters in their own hands. The lookout for a ninja and a kid with his face painted like a dead man is still in effect. Repeat: the lookout is still in effect. Twilight out."

"If any ghosts or goblins got to the thieves, it serves them right," Colt said as they started back for the car. "You steal, you pay."

"That's Willy Hynes talking," Twilight said. He held the pot of gold, "As 'Colt' you need to serve the law and the law applies to everyone, including supernaturals. If they attack the thieves, we have to arrest them."

"Yeah, yeah, I know," Colt said. "So what can we…"

Colt's sentence was cut off when he looked to the sky behind Twilight in awe. Curious as to what his apprentice was seeing, Twilight turned around and watched as one of the gargoyles that they talked to earlier from Saint Roland's cathedral glided down to the parking lot.

Twilight opened the driver's door to the '57 Chevy and placed the pot of gold inside. Colt circled around the rear end as the gargoyle approached. Colt forgot which gargoyle it was, but Twilight recognized the gold loop earrings and the slightly arched back. Howie approached them.

"Hey, what's happening?" Twilight said.

I don't tink you wanna know," Howie said.

"What is it? Did you find the thieves? Did something bad happen to them?"

"Naw, me and da boys ain't found the tieves yet," Howie said. "But tere's some trouble at the *7-Eleven* on the corner of Elm and Sherwood. Tis guy in a monkey suit and crazy red hair is makin' a ruckus."

"What do you mean by 'ruckus'?" Colt said.

"Ahh, he's breakin' glass and sayin' how he wants some kinda' rum."

Twilight and Colt looked at each other, then back at Howie.

"Did he have green skin?" Twilight said, "And a lantern?"

"Yeah, tat's right," Howie said. "You know, I ain't never seen him 'round here before. He kinda' looks like my tird cousin, Francisco, who watches over tis church in Sicily. Boy, tat Francis could play cards. He was a master at Blackjack and Five-Card Stud. I remember tis one time…"

The '57 Chevy roared out of the parking lot. Twilight and Colt had bolted into the vehicle right after Howie confirmed that the *7-Eleven* fiend was green-skinned and carried a lantern. The story about Howie's third cousin from Sicily had to wait. By the time Howie realized what was going on, the car was headed north. He was alone in Trevor Wallace Memorial Field's parking lot.

"YOU'RE WELCOME!" he said.

CHAPTER
40

Jadeite rode his skateboard down Enfield Street. His black and green cape flapped behind him as if it was trying to blend in with the surrounding darkness and wave at the nearby trick-or-treaters at the same time. The wind blew through his dirty blond hair as he looked left and right for any unusual activity. He only saw the usual residents: skeletons, nurses, *WWE* superstars, black cats, cheerleaders, and punk rockers. All of them were under five feet-seven inches and held bags of treats as they laughed and filled the night with their high-pitched chatter while their neon orange and green glow-sticks danced in the air.

The grumbling sound of the skateboard's wheels lowered as Jadeite slowed down. A trick-or-treater caught his attention. It wasn't a friend of his, nor was the costume that outrageous. The outfit was shabby. It was made up of black sweats and a face paint job that was melting as it mixed with sweat. It was a boy of about twelve or maybe fourteen at the oldest. He walked as if he had an "accident" in his pants. As he approached, Jadeite looked in the boy's blue eyes.

The lights are on, Jadeite thought, but no one's home.

Ordinarily, the Pniese do everything they can to stay out of the Living's business. If kids want to spray a house or car with shaving cream or toilet paper some trees, that was their prerogative. The Pniese were about maintaining law and order to the supernaturals. This boy, however, seemed too zoned out to ignore.

Jadeite held up his palm like a traffic cop. "Hold it."

The boy with the painted face never laid eyes on Jadeite and walked past him as if Jadeite were a cricket singing at his feet.

Jadeite rolled past the dazed boy and held out both palms this time. "Hold on a second, dude, I just want to talk to you."

The boy with the painted face hobbled past him.

Jadeite caught up with him the second time and grabbed the boy by the shoulders. "Dude, you okay?"

The boy said nothing. His eyes stared past Jadeite's white eye slits. His mouth hung open. Jadeite noticed one thing: the boy's face was painted like a skull. He took a closer look at the boy and made a memory match.

"Bobby McHooley, is that you?"

Bobby didn't answer. A string of saliva came out of the corner of his mouth.

Jadeite reached for his walkie-talkie, still holding Bobby in place with his other hand, and pressed the "talk" button. "This is Jadeite. I think I've caught one of the thieves that lifted Darby's gold. It's Bobby McHooley, but he's acting all funny. Over."

There was a buzz of static and then Moonbeam's voice came through the walkie-talkie. "What do you mean by 'funny?' Over."

Jadeite pressed the "talk" button again. "I mean he's all spaced out. He could be on something, but he doesn't smell bad or have any bloodshot eyes or anything. He's just got this empty look on his face. Over."

"Is he ignoring you and kinda walking like a zombie?" Moonbeam said in his static voice, "Over."

"Totally," Jadeite said.

"Is he heading in the direction of Raven River?"

"Ding," Jadeite said. "What's this all about? Over."

"I think our friend ran into Jack," Moonbeam said. "Just give him a light tap across his face, see if that helps. Over."

Jadeite took Moonbeam's advice. He ran his palm into Bobby McHooley's cheek with a crisp "smack." Bobby blinked into consciousness and looked around. "This ain't Trevor Wallace Field."

Jadeite turned his attention back to the walkie-talkie. "It worked. Over."

"Good," said Moonbeam. "Stay alert though. We got a few leads, but Pandusa is still on the loose. Over."

"If there's any more information I can get, I'll let all units know. Jadeite over and out."

"Yo, *Green Lantern*," Bobby McHooley said, "You wanna tell me what's going on around here? How did I end up way out here? And where's Daryl? Did he go home?"

Jadeite put his hefty arm around Bobby. "Dude, you and me are going to have a nice talk. I want to know everything you were doing before you blacked out."

CHAPTER 41

Poltergeist Prison was easy to spot if one was to take a ferry to the Netherworld, where all supernaturals return after their curfew on Halloween night. It was located on the Netherworld's dark side where the sky was always black regardless of whether it was clear or precipitating. The trees were always leafless and fog tingled along the ground.

If one were to get off the ferry, like Angel did, one would have to follow the long and entwined path up the hill. The building and its iron gates could be seen across the morbid countryside like a macabre antenna. Poltergeist Prison is the place where the supernatural world dumps its worst nightmares: an abode for the malevolent, the murderous, and the remorseless. The only place worse is the Devil's Domain.

Angel was tense as she walked the corridor with Nefrekhamen, Poltergeist Prison's warden. Warden Nefrekhamen was dressed from head to toe in tattered brown bandages. Bracelets gripped his wrists and several necklaces, one of which held many keys, hid much of his scrawny chest. A cane helped him with his walk as he limped along side the Monster Cop. All of Nefrekhamen's possessions were made of gold, which like silver, had a reputation of being effective protection against evil.

"You realize this is highly unusual," he said in his Egyptian accent.

"Yes, I know," Angel said, "but it's very important."

"I imagine so," Nefrekhamen said. "I've heard of this fellow, Jack. My people at the Nile said that they saw him once wandering the desert over a century ago. He truly does get around."

"He truly doesn't have a choice," Angel said. "Until recently that is."

"If I can help, I will," Nefrekhamen said. "And I'll make sure any inmate gives you any information you need."

"It's not information I'm looking for. It's a favor."

"A favor?" Nefrekhamen said. They approached the door to the maximum-security wing, "My dear, the type of monsters that reside in this area don't do favors."

"This one will," Angel said. She narrowed her white eyes in disgust when she thought of this particular prisoner.

Nefrekhamen took one of the gold keys from one of his many necklaces and opened the iron door to the forbidden wing. Two officers, both wearing security outfits and armed with holy water rifles stood before them. Angel's heart skipped a beat as her hand slapped her chest. The guards' heads and hands were without flesh. They were in a sense, walking skeletons.

"I'm sorry, Angel," said Nefrekhamen. "You'll have to leave your weapons here as a precautionary. I'm sure you understand."

"Yes, of course."

The skeleton guard on her left extended his hand and opened his bony fingers. Angel understood what he wanted. She handed him her bow. She then unhooked her quiver and handed that over as well. Her holy water squirt gun followed. She and Warden Nefrekhamen then threw their hands in the air and let the skeleton guards pat them down for hidden weapons or anything inappropriate to bring into the heart of the maximum-security wing. When they were clean, they continued down the corridor, lit by black candles. The candles were stuck in silver candlesticks that were attached to the stone walls. They were decorated with thick spider webs.

Angel noticed a pentagram on the floor up ahead, written in chalk. Its point was pointing away from them. The pentagram was used as a seal to make sure the evil ahead stayed in its designated place. Angel and the warden passed it with no problem. Beyond the pentagram was a large transparent wall that resembled thick plastic, but was made of an alien substance. On the other side of the transparent wall was a three-sided room made of stone. An iron door stood on the left side of its opposite wall.

Nefrekhamen limped up to the intercom on the transparent wall's left side. He pressed a red button. "Bring in Punchinello."

"Yes, sir," a static voice in the intercom said.

Angel took a deep breath. She felt both fright and anger at the inmate who was about to re-enter her life under grave circumstances. Yet, she was the one who had the advantage. After all, Punchinello owed her and he was going to pay tonight whether he liked it or not.

"I'll leave you two alone," Nefrekhamen said. "Don't get too close to the clear wall. If there's any problem, give us a yell and I'll have guards on both sides of the wall before you can blink twice."

"I appreciate that," Angel said. "Thank you, Nefrekhamen."

He nodded. "Anything to help."

The mummy warden hobbled across the great pentagram seal and made his way out of the maximum-security wing, his golden cane leading the way. Less than a minute later, the iron door on the other side of the transparent wall squealed open. Two skeleton guards entered. They walked backward with their holy water rifles drawn. The demon Punchinello followed in silver shackles. He saw Angel and gave a sick grin with his ruby bright lips, purple gums, and sharp yellow teeth.

"Hey, doll," he said, "miss me already?"

The silver chains rattled as Punchinello approached the transparent wall to get a better look at the one that arrested him two years ago. He was small in height, a mere five feet-four inches, but he weighed around three-hundred pounds. Not that Punchinello was muscular, quite the opposite. He was hunchbacked. His bulging stomach was the most noticeable part of his body, even though he had many other physical trademarks. Among such trademarks was his greasy white-skinned head that was bald on top with tufts of blue hair on the sides. Above his poisonous and snake-like yellow eyes were thin black eyebrows that sloped downwards and looked as if they were drawn on by a mascara pencil. His white nose looked like a toucan's beak. He was dressed in a one-piece red and white striped clown suit, complete with a ruffled collar, green pom-pom buttons, and the kind of white gloves that *Bugs Bunny* wore. To Angel, Punchinello looked like a cross between *Batman*'s nemesis the *Penguin* and a lost member of the music group, the *Insane Clown Posse*.

"You got those braces off, huh?" he said. The tip of his long nose touched the transparent wall.

"This isn't a reunion," Angel said. "I need something and you're going to get it for me."

"Oh really?" Punchinello said, "What do you need, doll? Another sweetheart?"

A low chuckle came out of his mouth as he watched Angel's face turn pink. Her teeth grind together. It didn't take much to get her riled up and for good reason.

"Go to Hell," she said, "and I mean that literally."

"Little too hot for my taste, doll," he said. "What do you want?"

"A piece of coal, blessed by the Devil himself," Angel said. "Warden Nefrekhamen says he'll allow you to cross the bridge between Poltergeist Prison and the Devil's Domain. When you arrive, you will find your master and tell him that the piece of coal he gave his old friend, Jack, has burned out and needs to be replaced. You will then proceed to come back here and hand the coal over to me and you'll do it in record time."

Punchinello fell silent for a few seconds.

Then he smiled.

And laughter stuttered out of his throat.

The demon clown threw his head back and nearly fell over as he laughed. He then hunched forward and gave the transparent wall in front of him a pound with his gloved fist, still roaring. The punch vibrated the clear wall and startled Angel for a moment. She refocused her disgust.

"I take it you're not in the mood for cooperating?"

Punchinello's laughter morphed into chuckling as he squashed his nose against the clear wall again. "You crack me up, doll. Should I bring back pizza while I'm at it? Or would you like Chinese instead?"

"Listen, you tub of crap," Angel said. "I'm not asking you. You're gonna to do what I tell you. So how do you want it? The easy way or the hard way?"

"And what's the hard way?" Punchinello said, "You can't do nothing to me anymore. I'm all locked up in this hole. You can't make my situation any worse."

"You wanna bet?" Angel said, "Me and Warden Nefrekhamen will make sure the Devil finds out that Jack isn't walking the Earth anymore. This guy, Jack, gave your master a whole lot of embarrassment and grief and if he finds out that you knew Jack was free and refused to cooperate with us, he's going to bring you home and punish you like you've never been punished before."

Punchinello's bloody grin shrunk. He lifted his nose from the transparent wall, which left behind a grease stain. He took a couple of steps back and emit a low snarl. "You're bluffing."

"Am I? You care to find out? Believe me, nothing would bring a smile to my face more than knowing you'll be roasting down there with brimstone suffocating your every pathetic breath. Remember, I had you right where I wanted you."

Her white-gloved finger tapped against the clear wall, aimed at Punchinello's stomach. "But I spared your life and that's a lot more than you deserve. You owe me big time. Now get me that coal or you're gonna suffer big time!"

Moonbeam and Specter didn't find any more stone statues of Sleepy Owl's residents. They searched the entire southern part of town to no avail. Pandusa the gorgon seemed further away than the planet, Neptune.

"What time is it?" Specter said, her body still transparent.

Moonbeam, still mounted on Phantom, peeled back part of his gray glove to his wrist. He felt his Braille watch.

"Nearly nine o' clock," he said. "I say we go back to town square and start spreading the word to the supernaturals that their time is almost up."

"What are we going to tell Pandusa's parents?" Specter said.

"The truth, what else?" Moonbeam said, "We still have a few hours before the veil closes up. We'll find her."

"Let's hope so," Specter said.

Suddenly, Specter stopped walking. She turned east and got on her knees.

Phantom trotted along and further distanced he and Moonbeam from their fellow Pniese. Specter put her hands together in a prayer position, fingers pointing up. She ordered Phantom to stop before she closed her eyes.

Phantom, with a whinny, halted in his place.

"Why are we stopping?" Moonbeam said with one hand gripping the end of his silver staff, "We're not in danger, are we?"

"No," Specter said.

"Do you see Pandusa?"

"No."

Moonbeam listened for anything unusual. He heard a car from two streets away and the rustling of tree branches. There was also faint gossip from the last of the season's crickets. "There aren't any trick-or-treaters coming our way are there?"

"Shoosh!"

"What is going on?" Moonbeam said, "Why are we stopping?"

"I'm doing something."

"What?"

"Praying for guidance."

"Praying for guidance?" Moonbeam said, "With all due respect, clues to finding a gorgon don't just drop from the sky."

Specter was about to counter her friend's remark when a solid mass from above plunged toward the ground less than twenty-five feet away.

The object crashed onto a nearby roof, then rolled down the slanted top and landed in rhododendron bushes, inches away from the house's foundation. Lucky for Moonbeam and Specter, no one was home. Otherwise, one would have stepped outside to investigate the commotion.

"What was that?" Moonbeam said, almost afraid to get an answer.

"Perhaps a clue that dropped from the sky," Specter said. "Let's take a closer look. It's in Mr. Greel's front yard."

Specter and Phantom trespassed onto Mr. Greel's deserted property. They strode up to the shrubs where the large object lay. When Specter got close enough, she saw that the object was actually a gargoyle frozen in flying position.

"It's one of our allies," Specter said. "I think it's Arullus from Saint Roland's cathedral."

Moonbeam got off of Phantom's back and made his way over to Specter and the bushes. He felt along the leaves until his fingers tapped against the hard surface that was Arullus's chest. He took off his glove and felt the hard surface once more.

"Stone," Moonbeam said. "Do you know what this means?"

Suddenly, it dawned on Specter as she snapped her finger.

"If he changed to stone in mid air just above us—"

"Then Pandusa is probably in the area," Moonbeam said. He took a deep breath and called out. "Pandusa! PANDUSA!"

Specter joined in. She cupped her hands and called for the child gorgon to come forth.

CHAPTER
43

The police, the kind that deals with the living, arrived at the corner of Elm and Sherwood before Twilight and Colt did. The patrol car's brakes squealed as they halted in front of the *7-Eleven*. Officers Skyler and Alben stepped out of the vehicle with their nightsticks ready. Officer Skyler was in his early thirties with a dark moustache. Officer Alben was in his late thirties, but looked older because of the crow's feet wrinkles around his eyes.

"You go on back," he said to Officer Skyler, "I'll get the front."

"Check," Officer Skyler said. He jogged to the *7-Eleven*'s left side and headed for his destination.

Officer Alben approached the building. As he got closer, he stepped on glass shards. The double doors and the huge windows on both sides of the *7-Eleven* were smashed. The sign on the right window that said, "Hot Dogs, 99 cents" was torn in half. Officer Alben heard a man grunting and more glass breaking inside the convenience store. He put his baton away and took out his pistol.

"Attention in there!" he said. "This is the police! I want you to come out with your hands up!"

"SAWD OFF!" the voice inside said.

Officer Alben took a deep breath and crept up to the double doors. Glass diamonds crunch beneath his shoes. He grabbed hold of the C-shaped metal door handle and tugged it open.

The inside was in shambles.

The bread and cereal shelf in front of him was knocked over, crashed on top of the canned food aisle. The glass doors on the frozen food display case against the right wall were shattered. Dozens of boxed entrées, ice cream containers, pizzas, popsicles, and bags of ice littered the floor. The refrigerator display case had the only glass door that was still intact, but the door itself was wide open. Icy steam escaped and mingled with the store's odor, which smelled like the inside of a pickle jar.

Officer Alben turned to the sales counter. He heard the radio, some talk show from Albertus Magnus College in New Haven. A body was sprawled over the cash register, its back to Officer Alben. It looked to be the body of a young man. Officer Alben reached for the CB that was attached to his shoulder lapel. He pressed the "talk" button, but before he could speak, a bright blue light shined in front of him.

"I said to sawd off!"

It was Jack. Somehow, he had sneaked up and managed to shove his lantern into Officer Alben's face like a newly engaged-woman showing off her diamond ring. Officer Alben fell under Jack's power. He obeyed the command given to him as he turned around and walked out of the store. As Officer Alben stepped out of the *7-Eleven*, his eyes empty of emotion, Officer Skyler came around the corner with his gun drawn.

"There's no one in the back," he said. "Alben? Are you okay? Alben?"

Officer Alben ignored his partner and headed for the street, unaware of where he was going. All he knew was to follow the orders given to him: to sawd off.

A bag of dog food hurled through the shattered right window. It struck Officer Skyler in his arm and shoulder. The bag tore. Hundreds of hard brown pellets shot out in every direction.

When the bag hit its target, Officer Skyler's gun went off.

The bullet whizzed across Sherwood Road and hit a telephone pole wire next to the woods. The wire snapped in two and both ends fell to the street. Wild sparks and electric-zapping sounds drown out the college radio talk show, even though it was two hundred feet away from the convenient store.

Officer Skyler made the natural and horrible mistake of looking to his right and into the *7-Eleven* to see who his attacker was. Jack stood on the other side of the window. He held his lantern up to Officer Skyler's face. Skyler's pupils shrunk. His mouth hung open and his conscious mind submitted to the ghoulish figure that was before him.

"Put your toy away and get lost!" Jack said.

Officer Skyler slid his gun back into his holster and walked away. He strolled past the police car he and Officer Alben drove in minutes ago.

Jack turned around as well, going deeper into the store to find more rum. Among the many empty bottles on the floor, he managed to find one that hadn't been broken or opened. His misshapen lips were ready to drink again, when he heard another car pull up.

"I've got to learn to pay for things," Jack said.

Twilight and Colt got out of their 1957 Chevy with their holy water guns drawn.

"Remember if it's him, don't look into the lantern," Twilight said.

"I know," Colt said.

"I'm serious," Twilight said.

"I know!" Colt said, "Let's just get the guy!"

Their plan of going in to attack wouldn't be necessary. Jack opened the left glass door. He looked more aggravated than ever. His orange eyes seemed twice as large as a normal person's and his frown would probably give an older man a heart attack. He had one of his hands behind his back.

"So there's more of ya, is there?" he said.

"Put your hands up, Jack," Twilight said. "It's all over."

"Oh no lad, tis just beginning. You ever walk a great distance, have ya? Do ya remember how much pain you got in your knees and feet? Well that's nothing compared to my pain. It got to a point where I couldn't feel anything from the waist down. Trust me, lad, no one is going to force me to do anything ever again so ya may as well put down your wee weapons."

"Not a chance," Twilight said.

Colt took out his silver handcuffs. He held one bracelet in his red-gloved hand and shook the dangling chain and other bracelet, causing a light jingling sound. "Lookee what I got."

"Ya just don't listen, do ya?" Jack said.

He brought the hand from behind his back to the front. It held the lantern. Jack stepped forward to give it a closer display.

"TURN AWAY!" Twilight said, "DON'T LOOK INTO IT!"

Colt zipped behind the police car and fired his squirt gun. Lines of holy water shot out and hit Jack in the face and hands. The entity wailed, but was still on his feet and still held the lantern. Colt's holy water assault, however, caused Jack to get distracted enough for Twilight to run up and knock the lantern out of Jack's hand.

Jack was quick to react. Almost instantly, he wrapped his hands around Twilight's neck and leaned forward, causing Twilight's back to land on the police car's hood.

Colt circled around the front of the cruiser and attempted to aid his mentor. Jack backhand-slapped Colt and sent him to the pavement. Blood dripped from Colt's nose.

With only one hand on his throat, Twilight was able to break free and punch Jack in the jaw. Jack stumbled back. He shook his head, trying not to let the sting get to him. Twilight aimed his squirt gun. He almost pulled the trigger, but Jack was fast enough to snatch it away. With one hand on the grip and the other on the nozzle, Jack broke the squirt gun in half like a turkey wishbone. Blue plastic shards fell to the ground and holy water sprayed in all directions. Jack felt pain from the water, but refused to let his enemies know it.

For a few seconds, no one attacked. The only noises heard were the college talk show coming from the radio inside the convenient store and the live wire's steady popping and zapping across the street.

Colt got up from the ground and noticed that when he fell, his red squirt gun had cracked as well. Jack also appeared to have noticed his advantage. His lantern was only a few feet away from him, but he chose not to go for it. The Monster Cops couldn't stop him, but they did hurt him and now it was time for them to pay.

He grinned. A putrid steam of breath exhaled out of him. He held up his fists.

Twilight stared for a second then looked through the broken left window and noticed the cashier, lying motionless on top of his register. He turned to Colt. "Go inside the store and see if the cashier needs medical help."

"But I can get the lantern," Colt said. "If we destroy it, this jerk won't be able to hurt anyone anymore."

"I'll worry about that," Twilight said. "People come first, Colt. Now move."

Colt hesitated for a second and then opened the right double door.

"You have no idea what you're up against," Jack said.

"Bite me," Twilight said.

Jack battle cried and charged forward, fist first. Twilight ducked and returned the favor with a shot to the side of Jack's ribs, followed by another punch to the jaw. Jack was still on his feet. Twilight grabbed Jack's coat and pulled back his blue-gloved fist for a knockout punch. Jack shifted his body and flipped the Monster Cop over. Twilight did a one-eighty in mid air and landed on his back on the police car's hood again, his black hair brushed against Jack's stomach. A metallic thud echoed in the air.

Inside the store, Colt lowered his head. The cashier had no pulse. Judging by the bruises on his neck, it looked as if Jack had strangled the poor guy to death. He turned his attention to the rest of the store and began to search for anything unusual…well, more unusual than usual. His red combat boots crunched wherever they stepped as open cereal boxes, broken bottles, metal nuts, and bolts from the now demolished slushy machine lay on the floor.

"What a bender he must have thrown," Colt said.

He went past the candy and magazine shelves. At the end of the aisle, he saw the refrigerator case. Bottles and cans of soda, *Gatorade*, *Yoo-Hoo*, spring water, and a variety of juice drinks cluttered the floor. Most of the clear containers leaked and caused all the beverages to mix together and form a sticky, wide, carbonated, soupy brown puddle. His boots made a swishing sound when he got closer. Outside, he heard Jack and Vince curse and wail as they plunged into heavy combat. Colt picked up the walkie-talkie from his belt and pressed the "talk" button.

"Attention everyone," he said, "Jack is at the *7-Eleven* on the corner of Sherwood and Elm. Him and Twilight are going at it, but I don't know how long we can hold. We need backup a.s.a.p., aaaright? Colt out."

He put his walkie-talkie back on his belt and kicked his way through the bottles and cans. He headed left to check the remaining aisles. Colt found one other person in the hygiene section. It was easy to see why Colt couldn't have detected him sooner. The young man stood still and expressionless. Colt recognized him when he saw the red hair and freckled face. From the neck down, the kid was dressed as a ninja, but in Tae Kwon Do, he only made yellow belt. It was Willy Hynes's friend,

Daryl Julson.

Daryl didn't notice Colt approaching him. He kept staring at the shelf in front of him, specifically, a bag of *Ruffles* potato chips. Daryl's mouth hung open. The black ninja hood had probably blown away back at the Trevor Wallace Memorial Field.

Colt stood in front of Daryl. He couldn't help but smirk. "Oh, how it just pains me to do this."

He slapped Daryl across the face.

Daryl blinked into consciousness and looked around.

"Hey, how did I get here?" he said then noticed the kid in the black outfit with the red mask, "Who are you? Where's Bobby?"

"It figures you'd be with McHooley," Colt said. "Every time you do, something bad happens: You get detention, you get hurt, a drunk hypnotizes you. Come on, let's go out the back door."

"Wait, who are you?" Daryl said, "And why don't we go out the front?"

Colt took Daryl's arm and led him to the end of the aisle. He showed Daryl the *7-Eleven*'s broken windows and double doors. Beyond that, Daryl saw a guy dressed like Colt except his outfit was black and blue, fighting another guy in a cheap suit with green skin and large eyes.

"That's why," Colt said.

Twilight had a fat lip. His back was sore from slamming onto the police cruiser. Jack was just as hurt with a broken nose and a missing tooth. His maroon blood dripped down one end of his mouth and both nostrils. Still, both combatants had no desire to wane in their brawl. They had given each other their best shots. Though they were dizzy and the pain from such blows started to set in, both still had the desire to win. Jack took a few steps back from Twilight and then punched a hole through the police car's passenger side window. When he brought his hand out, he held a large triangular piece of glass. His hand was bleeding from the impact, but his expression was gleeful.

"Come on, lad," he said. "Ya ready for round two?"

Jack didn't wait for an answer. He charged with the clear blade leading the way.

Twilight focused on the weapon. At the last second, he stepped out of the way and used Jack's momentum against him as he shoved his enemy. Jack lost his balance and tumbled to the ground. The dingy top hat came off his head. He was a few inches away from the convenience store's double doors. No sooner when he got up, Jack was knocked down once more. Twilight had given him a spinning heel kick. Jack's left eye tingled with soreness. His vision was blurred. He tried to get up again, but the cobwebs in his brain didn't permit it without time to recuperate.

"All right, lad," he said and extended his arms outward. "Ya got me. I do hope you're happy, I do."

"Thrilled," Twilight said. He took out his silver handcuffs and stepped forward. He leaned down to put the braces on the green wrists, when Jack suddenly struck him in the heart.

For an instant, Twilight couldn't talk or breathe. It was short-lived as Jack gave him an uppercut and sent him sailing onto his back, this time on the pavement instead of the police car's hood. Jack staggered to his feet. His smile was a mixture of oil brown teeth and maroon blood that dripped down his chin.

"When ya live for at least two lifetimes," he said to the groaning Twilight, "ya learn to become a notorious, yet highly believable liar. I thought it would be fun to fight ya I did, but now I think I should get me lantern and finish up."

Jack looked to his left. The lantern was still on its side and glowing its turquoise light between Twilight's '57 Chevy and a pay phone that was just passed the store's right display window. He took no more than two steps when he heard a light metallic stuttering click and a pull from his left wrist. He looked down at his hand. Colt had handcuffed him to one of the door handles.

"Why you little—"

Colt took a few steps away and pointed. "Yeah!"

He raised his fists to the sky and hopped up and down like a boxer that just won the World Heavyweight title. "Who the man? Who the man!"

As Colt jumped up and down, he shifted his body and attention away from Jack. That was all the opportunity the green-skinned entity needed. With a loud grunt, he thrust his foot at the lower half of Colt's cape.

Colt toppled to the ground. He wailed as he held his right knee.

"Willy!" Twilight said.

A newfound strength surfaced within him. He got to his feet, ran over, and slugged Jack. The punch was powerful enough to almost send Jack through one of the double doors.

"If you've hurt him, I'm gonna—"

"It's cool," Colt said, though the pain could be detected in his voice. "I'm okay."

Colt tried to get up. He almost reached his full height when his injured knee gave in. He tumbled to the parking lot. A grunt through grinding teeth. "Ah crap."

"Does it feel broken?" Twilight said as he approached his student.

"I don't know," Colt said. "He might have just blown out my knee."

"What were you thinking?" Twilight said.

"What do you mean?"

"I mean what was all that bouncing around and celebrating? Especially when you were within his range? You're lucky all he did was kick you."

"And you're lucky I cuffed him," Colt said. "I noticed *you* couldn't get it done, so back off, aaaright?"

"Listen you, don't confuse skill with dumb luck," Twilight said. "You can't be going into battle like you're in some Will Smith movie." Twilight pointed to Jack who was sitting down and enjoying their quarrel. "He would've broken every bone in your body if given half the chance."

"That's true," Jack said.

"Shut up!" Twilight and Colt said at the same time.

"What do you want me to say? That I'm sorry?" Colt said, "All right! I'm sorry! I'm completely frickin' sorry! But we got him! So just go in the Monster-mobile, play some James Brown or whatever, and keep away from me cause I ain't in the mood to be playin' aaaright?"

Jack looked at the black '57 Chevy. "You call that the Monster-mobile?"

"Shut up!" Twilight and Colt said.

They looked back to each other.

"Look, I am the teacher, you are the student," Twilight said. "What I say—"

"Saints preserve us!"

An Irish-accented voice made its presence known. Darby the leprechaun stood at the corner of the convenience store, his hands on his small hips.

Twilight waved to him. "We found your gold."

"Aye, I know," Darby said. "I bumped into Jadeite in town square. He went and showed me the young bugger who took me gold. At least one of them. The one with the painted face."

Darby waddled closer to the Pniese warriors, but to do so meant going past Jack. Although Jack was sitting and appeared sedated, Twilight was going to take no chances. He held up his hand.

"Don't get too close," he said. "He's dangerous."

Darby kept his distance, but couldn't help leaning forward to take a closer look at the prisoner. Darby took off his green derby and scratched his red-haired skull while his green eyes squinted. "Now what manner o' creature is this?"

"They don't have a name for him," Twilight said then turned to Colt. "Go get the gold."

"Yeah, aaaright," Colt said. He limped his way over to the vehicle.

Darby put his lid back on. Jack grinned at him. Darby stared back for a pause then shook his head, his jowls vibrating. "You're an ugly one, ya are."

Jack continued to smile wide and let out a snicker.

"Don't irritate him, Darby," Twilight said. "It's been a long night and cuffing him took a lot out of me and Colt."

"Speak for yourself, old timer," Colt said. He shut the '57 Chevy's passenger side door. The pot of gold was in his red-gloved hand, "You may have gotten knocked around, but ain't nothing but a thing for yours truly."

"Get over yourself," Twilight said.

"Hey, I just want credit where credit is due," Colt said. "Would it kill you to say, 'Hey Colt, you the man'?"

"It's your first night," Twilight said. "No one becomes the man overnight."

"Says who?"

"Says me. I also say you got a chip on your shoulder."

"And I say I don't need you watching my every move! Who's the prisoner here, me or Jack?"

Darby could see that the arguing among the Pniese was heating up. In a situation like this, he thought it best if he took back his gold and crept away. It was getting late anyway. Many of the supernaturals were returning to the Netherworld, a place that sounded more attractive at this moment.

Darby waddled in Colt's direction then fell to the ground.

The sound of Darby's upper body hitting the pavement caught Colt and Twilight's attention. Darby's stocking ankle was on top of one of Jack's. This gave Twilight the quick assumption that Darby got too close and allowed Jack to trip him.

Colt dropped the pot of gold. Twilight started to close in on Darby, when Jack grunted and yanked his captured arm. The handcuffs' silver chain snapped. Jack scooped up Darby and rose to his feet.

"Let me go, you wicked scoundrel!" Darby said. His brass-buckled shoes kicked the air and hit Jack in the belly. Unfortunately for Darby, the strength in his heels weren't considerable enough to cause damage. He felt Jack's arms wrap around his throat and his stomach.

"Let him go, Jack!" Twilight said.

"Anything you say," Jack said, using the leprechaun as a shield. He made his way over a few more feet and with the shuffle of his hands, Jack managed to pick up his lantern. He held it up in front of Darby.

"Oh no," Twilight half-whispered.

Darby was under Jack's spell. His bearded jaw fell and his pupils closed in from gazing at the robin's egg blue light. Everyone fell silent for a few seconds. All that was heard was the buzzing and popping of the live wires across the street whose cut ends still bounced on the road and spit out yellow and blue sparks. Twilight felt his stomach churn when he saw that Jack had noticed the live wires and smiled.

"I think you need a little shock therapy," he said in Darby's ear.

Darby managed a slight nod. Jack set the leprechaun down. Twilight and Colt watched in horror as Darby began to waddle past the cars and head across the street where he and the live wires would become electrically acquainted.

"Darby, no!" Twilight took a few steps in the leprechaun's direction.

Jack laughed. "Choices, choices. What's it going to be, lad? Me or the runt?"

"Keep an eye on him," Colt said to Twilight, "I'll get Darby!"

Colt started to chase after the leprechaun. His limp was slowing him down and Darby had too much of a head start. Twilight watched. Colt was catching up with Darby, but slowly…much too slowly.

"I'm coming!" Twilight said.

Colt turned his head to Twilight, still limping and held up his gloved hand. "No! Stay with him! I can do this! Please!"

Twilight felt as if he were a rope in the middle of a tug of war between two trucks. His legs shook with anticipation and begged for action. When he looked at Jack, all he saw was the monster's hideous grin as laughter sputtered out of his throat.

"Me or the runt, lad?" Jack said. He picked up his top hat and dusted it off. "Don't you think I'm worth the life of a meaningless pipsqueak? Hmmm?"

Twilight balled up his fists. He wanted to hit Jack with everything he had, but if this encounter taught him anything, it was that Jack didn't fall easily. Instead, he slammed his fists on the '57 Chevy's roof and ran in Darby's direction. When he whizzed past the limping Colt, he heard his student shout out, "YOU IDIOT!"

Darby was within six feet of the live wires. Consciously, he ignored the danger he was in. Subconsciously, he tried to fight with his willpower, to turn back, to snap out of the terrible trance he had been put in.

It was futile.

He would touch the wire. Lightning and unspeakable agony would whip up and down his body. His hair would catch fire, his body would shake, and the torture would go on too long before he would succumb. He leaned down and extended his hand. A spark bounced off his palm, giving him an appetizer for things to come.

That is, until Twilight grabbed Darby's arms and pulled him back.

He spun Darby around and gave him a slap. Darby had come to after a few blinks. "Wha—wha happened? Where's that ugly guy? Did I get me gold?"

Twilight and Darby crossed the street, heading back to the convenient store parking lot. Colt leaned his back on the '57 Chevy with his arms crossed and a tone of red in his skin that almost matched his mask. Jack was gone. Twilight and Darby collected the coins that Colt dropped on the ground and placed them back into the crock.

"Thank ya kindly, to the both of you," Darby said, then leaned towards Twilight. "It looks like your Colt will do after all."

Twilight didn't respond. He asked Darby to excuse he and Colt and further encouraged him to head for the woods where he could return to the Netherworld. Darby agreed and was out of sight a minute later.

Colt tore his mask off and started to undo his cape.

"What are you doing?" Twilight said, not wanting to hear the answer.

"Halloween is over," Willy Hynes said. He rolled his black and red cape into a ball and threw it in the car. "Your legacy ends here."

"I had no choice. Darby would have been toast if I didn't get to him."

"You did have a choice!" Willy said, "You could've let me handle it like I asked…no, 'begged' you to! But no!"

"That's not fair. Could you guarantee that you would have gotten to him while I kept an eye on Jack?"

"Could you guarantee that I wouldn't have?"

"Will you calm down?"

"No, I won't calm down! Ever since I got involved with this, you haven't trusted me once! When are you gonna realize that I don't need a babysitter anymore!"

"When you start giving me a reason!" Twilight said, "Because you didn't pay attention to Jack, he injured your knee. What's it going to be next time? A concussion or getting paralyzed? Or something worse?"

"Then you should have told that Indian chief in my dream that you wouldn't train me as your replacement," Willy said. "I didn't ask for any of this! I'm not a relative of yours and I'm not doing this anymore because me getting involved with this is bringing out the idiot in you!"

"What's going on here?" a female voice said from behind them.

Angel skated into the parking lot. She was carrying a black stone box under her arm. "I could hear you two a mile away. Willy, what are you doing with your mask off?"

"Ask him," Willy pointed to Twilight. "While you're at it, ask him why he let Jack get away. I'm all done with this."

Willy took the seven-pointed silver-star badge off his chest. He tossed it inside the car on top of the Colt cape.

CHAPTER
44

All Pniese members, including Willy Hynes, were gone by the time more police arrived at the *7-Eleven* parking lot. They had jumped into the '57 Chevy and found more privacy at Sleepy Owl High School's parking lot on Clarmont Avenue. Jadeite met them there. He took Willy aside in hopes of straightening out the problem the former Colt had with his mentor.

"He's an idiot," Willy said. "He let Jack get away because he couldn't trust me enough."

"From what I heard, you got a little overconfident when it came to battling Jack," Jadeite said. "Sounds to me like Twilight had reason to be concerned about you. Wouldn't you have been if the roles were reversed?"

Willy thought about it for a moment. "Yeah, I guess so. But he still should have trusted me. I could've caught Darby in time."

"Maybe," Jadeite said. "Dude, what you have to remember is that he's the mentor and you're the apprentice. You did learn a lot from him, didn't you?"

Willy nodded. "Yeah, he had some good points, I know."

"Twilight has always tried to look out for each and every one of us over the last six years," Jadeite said. "The last thing he wants is for any of us to get hurt. Maybe this year, he's leaning extra hard on you because he knows that next year, he won't be able to get involved when you take his place."

"*If* I take his place."

"It's true that you've been burdened with a huge responsibility. He's been tough, but if I know Vince, he's also very fair. He could've flat out refused to train you if he really wanted to. But the elder warriors, the ones we all dreamt of, knew that you were worthy of this duty. More importantly, Vince knew deep down that you were worthy of this duty."

"Are you saying that I've got no right to be mad?" Willy said.

"No, you have the right," Jadeite said. "You can leave this mission and the next five Halloween missions if you want to. There isn't a single one of us that hasn't felt like doing that at one time or another. Dude, all I'm saying is if you're going to stick around, you have to learn to listen to those who have more experience than you. Remember, one day you'll have to train a Colt of your own."

Jadeite's last statement hit Willy hard. Though he wanted to continue to defend himself or reply with a sarcastic remark, no words came to him. For the first time, Willy put himself completely in Vince's shoes and understood that in some ways, he, Willy, may have been wrong.

"He's brash and hot-tempered," Twilight said.

He sat on the '57 Chevy's hood next to Angel. His arms were folded as he looked out at the clear sky and the twisted branches that tried to reach for it. Angel put her white-gloved hand on his shoulder.

"Who isn't at thirteen?"

"He doesn't know when to listen," Twilight said. "I told him a million times to never take his eyes off an enemy and look what he does. He gets his knee blown out. And then I'm the bad guy because I wanted to make sure that Darby didn't end up like a *Chicken McNugget*."

"He made a mistake," Angel said. "We all make mistakes, you included. Maybe he's angrier at the fact that you aren't showing him as much faith as you should. We've all noticed how hard you've been on him, but we try not to interfere because we know you mean well by doing so."

"There are a lot of reasons why I've been hard on him," Twilight said. "You want to hear a big one?"

"Okay."

Twilight took a deep breath and let it out slowly. "I keep thinking about last year. I keep thinking about how Jessey was in Willy's shoes and ended up in the emergency room. Then I remember how hard it was for Kitt to concentrate on the mission and how she blamed herself for so long. I swore that when it was my time to train a Colt, I wouldn't make the same mistakes she did."

"You've done a great job with Willy," Angel said. "He's fast and smart and strong, but you got to let him grow. You gotta realize that you won't be able to protect him at all times, not on Halloween or any other night."

She put her arm around him and squeezed. "You were a great leader. But this time, you're not the leader. I am. This time, your duty is to show him the ropes and pass the torch."

Twilight, like Willy, found himself silent. He knew that she was right. After a pause, he put his gloved hands on his face and let them slide down. "I just did what I thought was right. I figured that we could always catch Jack later on, but with Darby, there would have been no second chance."

"I don't know if the decision you made was right or wrong. I wasn't there at the time," Angel said. "What I can tell you is that if my Colt told me that he could've caught Darby, I would've trusted his instincts… especially if my Colt was someone like Willy."

CHAPTER 45

Twilight and Willy Hynes were face to face by the '57 Chevy's headlights. Willy leaned on the hood. Twilight held the cape and mask that Willy wore earlier when he was known as "Colt." They didn't say anything at first, but the silence and hesitation proved too much to bear.

"You okay?" Twilight finally said.

"Yeah, I'm cool," Willy said. "How about you?"

"I'm a little sore from Jack's punches and what not, but I'm okay."

"Yeah," Willy said, "you were giving him the ol' one, two. Maybe you should've farted. That might've done it."

Twilight managed to smile.

A weak snicker came out of Willy as he extended his hands. "You want me to hold those?"

"Only if you want to," Twilight said. "I kind of got the feeling your Pniese career was over, even though it never really started and what not."

"Yeah, well," Willy said, "maybe I shouldn't have been so cocky… at certain times."

Twilight handed the cape and mask over. "Maybe I shouldn't have been so strict…at certain times. I'm sorry about not trusting you enough."

"Yeah, aaaright, I'm sorry too," Willy said. He took the garments, "Sincerely, this time. Despite what you think, I only wanted to make you proud. That's one of the biggest reasons I agreed to join your little club here."

"You've always made me proud," Twilight said. "I guess sometimes when I look at you, I think of Mike. It would kill me if I lost you too. I guess I was hoping that I could keep you out of danger and yet still have you take my place."

"I like taking risks. That's just the way I am. But I think I'm at the age where I know when to draw the line."

"I suppose you are," Twilight said. Another weak smile, "What do you say we finish this night and maybe see if your parents have any leftover candy?"

"Yeah, aaaright."

Willy placed the red raccoon-style mask on his face. His brown eyes were gone and white slits took their place. He was "Colt" again. He fastened his red and black cape around his neck. "Let's find Jack and get our rematch."

Twilight held up Colt's silver seven-pointed badge. He slightly rolled it between his gloved finger and thumb. "Don't forget this."

Jadeite had joined Angel at the vehicle's rear end. She took out her walkie-talkie and patted the small stone box that rested on top of the trunk with her white-gloved hand.

"What is this?" Jadeite said.

"The key to getting rid of our friend, Jack," she said then pressed the "talk" button on her walkie-talkie.

CHAPTER
46

"Oh, thank you!" Ariel the gorgon said to Moonbeam and Specter. She took her daughter, Pandusa, in her arms and squeezed. They reunited at town square, where the annual Halloween party was winding down. Over half of the townsfolk and supernaturals had gone back to their abodes.

Moonbeam and Specter had found Pandusa on Acorn Street, near Littlefield Drive where Mr. Coogan was still lying on the side of the street, frozen in stone. After discovering the statue version of their ally, Arullus the gargoyle, they called out for Pandusa as loud as they could until the child gorgon answered in her squeaky voice.

"Here I am!" she said through the darkness.

"Where?" Moonbeam said.

"Here!"

"Where here?"

"Here!"

"That helps," Moonbeam said as Phantom trotted along.

"Pandusa, don't move!" Specter said, still in her transparent form. "Just keep talking and we'll track you down!"

"In fact, sing a song!" Moonbeam said.

"What kind of song?" Pandusa said in the distance.

"Any song!"

"Does rap count?"

"NO!" Moonbeam and Specter said together.

The young gorgon started to sing. "You know Dasher and Dancer and Prancer and Vixen, Comet and Cupid and Donner and Blitzen...but do you recall, the most famous reindeer of all?"

Specter rolled her eyes. "Even in the Netherworld, they promote Christmas before Halloween is over."

They traveled down Ivy Avenue and then made a short cut through the woods to Acorn Street where Pandusa's singing grew louder. Once they got to the middle of the road, they came across a small cemetery. The cemetery had eight plots and a tomb that had Ionic columns. All the graves dated back to the 1700s, when one could bury their relatives on their property. In this case, the land at that time belonged to a wealthy family called the Van Holden's, who were half-Dutch and half-Greek. Eventually, the entire family perished from disease and their land was up for grabs, but the new owners decided not to transfer the bodies to Sleepy Owl's official cemetery near town square. Instead, the homes on Acorn Street were built around the small graveyard.

Pandusa's Yuletide melody was coming from the tomb. As the Monster Cops drew closer, she came out from hiding behind one of the Ionic columns. She was hugging it with one arm.

"This place reminds me of home," she said.

Moonbeam got off of Phantom. He handed Pandusa her mandatory sunglasses. Specter skipped her wampum whip, returning her body into solid form. They were back in town square in less than fifteen minutes, where Herebus and Ariel waited for their daughter.

"You've done us a great service," Herebus said.

"It's all in a night's work," Specter said. "I'm just glad she wasn't hurt."

"Me too," Ariel said. "Pandusa, what do you say to our Pniese friends?"

"Thank you," the child gorgon said in a voice that was both high-pitched and cute.

"You're welcome," Moonbeam said. "Now you guys should start thinking about packing it in and—"

"Moonbeam, Specter, come in. Over." Angel's static message came from their walkie-talkies.

"I'll get it," Moonbeam said to Specter. He removed the walkie-talkie from his gray belt. "This is Moonbeam, go ahead. Over."

"Where are you? Over," Angel said.

"Town square," Moonbeam said. "We're enforcing the curfew. Over."

"Did you find the missing gorgon? Over."

"Mission accomplished. Over."

"Good. I need you and Specter to meet us at Donovan's Bridge. I think I have a way to stop Jack. Over."

"Really?" Moonbeam said, "How?"

The Pniese had dealt with enemies who were clever. The enemy even outsmarted them at times. Two years ago, Carnaby's Circus outsmarted them and almost wiped out the Pniese for good. Last year, Bloody Mary outsmarted Jessey Sassacus and sent her to the emergency room.

Jack didn't fit this description.

Although practically invincible, his mentality was feeble. When he saw the signs marked, "Voodoo Rum this way!" with an arrow pointing north, he believed they were genuine. For almost half a mile, Jack followed the "Voodoo Rum" signs. First, they were on Route 54. Then he had to turn right to an unpaved trail through the woods. His mouth watered. The thought of being intoxicated motivated him to pick up speed. He came to the trail's end and saw Donovan's Bridge.

The bridge connected Sleepy Owl to its neighboring town, Donovan's Grove. It was made of wood and wide enough to let one car cross over at a time. The guardrails were four feet high. Raven River flowed twenty feet below. Next to the bridge on the Sleepy Owl side was another sign: "VOODOO RUM ACROSS THE BRIDGE!"

Jack wasted no time. He hurried across the bridge, his hideous grin displayed in the lantern's blue light. As he was getting closer, Jack saw two large boulders at the end of the bridge, one in front of each post as if they were some kind of bizarre metal-detector one had to pass through before crossing into the next town. Next to the boulder on the right stood another sign, but not like the others, which were made with scrap wood and spray paint. This sign was white and metallic. It stood on a metal pole: "Welcome to Donovan's Grove. Population: 5783. Est. 1705." Jack could care less about the town's facts. If there was voodoo rum in this Donovan's Grove place, he was going to find it.

He heard the young man's voice from behind. "Yo!"

Jack turned around and saw Colt.

Colt kissed his gloved hand and then smeared it on his buttock.

Jack knew what that meant. He headed back into Sleepy Owl to take care of Colt once and for all, when he suddenly felt a tug at his wrists. He looked left and right. Twilight and Jadeite came out from behind the boulders that stood on the Donovan's Grove's side of the bridge. They had rope in their hands and it stretched to Jack's wrists. The Monster Cops had lassoed him. They made their way onto Donovan's Bridge.

On the other end of the bridge, Angel ran next to Colt with the stone box in her hands. She gave Colt a quick pat on his shoulder.

"Go!" she said. "Get the lantern and be careful!"

Colt limped across the bridge. He tried to ignore his leg pain and made sure that he didn't stare directly into Jack's lantern, which was still in his left hand. Twilight, who had lassoed Jack's left wrist, was being equally careful by looking away from the entity that had roughed him up earlier. As Colt raced closer, Jack struggled to break free. When Colt was close enough, Jack could only think of one alternative—he kicked Colt in the stomach, knocking the wind out of the amateur Pniese.

"Colt!" Twilight said.

The distraction was all Jack needed. With a quick yank, Twilight's rope snapped. Jack was partially free as a small line of rope dangled from his left wrist.

He turned his attention to Jadeite and held his lantern up.

Jadeite couldn't react in time. His eyes fixed on the luminous blue light. He was hypnotized almost instantly. The grip on his rope loosened.

"Into the river with ya!" Jack said.

Jadeite let go of his rope. He faced the wooden guardrail.

"Jadeite, don't!" Twilight said. He tackled Jack to the planked floor just as Jack pulled Jadeite's rope free from his wrist.

Twilight's plea went unanswered. Jadeite flung himself over the rail. He hit the water in seconds. When the huge splash he made settled, Angel noticed that he was sinking.

"No!" she said.

Angel set the stone box down by the end of the bridge, ripped off her black and white cape, and hurled herself over the guardrail. Unlike

Jadeite's pencil position when he flew down, Angel's dive was more athletic, going down those twenty exhilarating feet. When she hit the water, the frigidness stung for a few seconds. She paddled her way towards the zoned-out Jadeite as she listened to the water splash around her. Her teeth were already chattering.

On Donovan's Bridge, Twilight and Jack were into their rematch. They rolled around until Twilight's back pressed hard against the guardrail. Colt glanced at the fallen lantern. It was lying on its side near Jack's top hat. He picked it up. His knee throbbed, but he limped back to the other side of the bridge where the stone box that Angel put down waited. He came within a yard's distance of the stone container when his neck jolted back. Jack had grabbed his black and red cape and jerked. Colt hit the planked floor, back first.

"What have we here?" Jack said. He scooped up his lantern and eyed the black stone box. Colt felt an icy sweat drip down his forehead and under his arms as Jack picked up the box and opened the lid. Inside the stone box was a piece of coal. Red light blazed from it and made Jack's already ugly features all the more ghastly.

"Another hunk of coal for me?" Jack said. He looked down at Colt, who was still too sore to move. "But Santa, I've been so good this year!"

A laugh stammered out of him as he closed the lid to the stone box. "Not this time, lad!" He tossed the box into the river on the opposite side that Jadeite and Angel jumped from.

Colt felt himself get heavier. It was the kind of heaviness that came with failure. Jack continued to laugh. Whether it was in triumph or the attempt to imprison him again, Colt didn't know.

They heard footsteps on the bridge.

Jack turned around. Twilight punched him in the eye. Jack dropped his lantern again as fell down. Twilight took out his silver handcuffs and shackled Jack's wrists while the entity's thoughts were still swimmy.

"I gotta get that box," Twilight said.

"I'll do it," Colt said. "You gotta make sure he doesn't get away."

"Out of the question. You can barely walk, never mind swim. Plus, you can't hold your breath as long as you need to."

"I'll get the breathing helmet from the car! Please, you said you would trust me!"

"Colt, I—"

Twilight's sentence was cut off. Jack swept his leg. Twilight's boots flew upward as he fell on his side. Jack snapped the handcuff's chain and pounced on top of him.

Colt limped to the 1957 Chevy, which was parked a few yards away from the Sleepy Owl end of Donovan's Bridge. On the way, he took out a pair of keys from his pocket. One of the keys was to the trunk.

"Jadeite! Bill!" Angel swam closer.

The water was up to his green mask. He dunked under once, before his head resurfaced and bobbed in the water. When the river level reached his dirty blond hair, Angel snatched him under the chin and brought his face up to the surface. His teeth were chattering like hers. Her gloved hand slapped Jadeite's chubby face, welcoming him back to reality.

Jadeite hacked up water. "Did we get him? Jeez! This water's freezing!"

"Really? You don't say?" Angel said, "You wanna get out?"

"Oh, all right," Jadeite said. "My skin is starting to wrinkle anyway."

They swam for the hills.

Colt had limped back to Donovan's Bridge with the Breathalyzer helmet under his arm. The pain in his knee was getting worse. Jack was on top of Twilight, still fighting near the Sleep Owl end of the bridge. Colt planned to get past the green-skinned menace and then make a break for the water. He thought about going down to Raven River without jumping from the bridge, but the hills that stood before the water were too steep and rocky. If Colt stepped in the wrong place or slipped altogether, the momentum would send him hurling down in circles where he could crash into just about anything from rocks to tree trunks.

He drew closer to the battle, hearing Twilight and Jack's grunting as they tried to get the best of each other with sucker punches and wrestling holds. Jack seemed too focused on Twilight. That was good. As quietly and swiftly as he could, Colt limped past Jack and Twilight and made his way closer to the middle of the bridge. Colt breathed a sigh of relief and put on the Breathalyzer helmet. It embraced his head for no more than a few seconds when he heard Jack's roaring voice.

"NO YOU DON'T!"

The helmet was ripped off Colt's head. Colt turned around and saw Jack throw the Breathalyzer helmet to the ground and give it a few stomps. The loud cracking of thick plastic came from the headgear. Jack pulled back his fist, ready to hit Colt when Twilight bear-hugged him from behind.

"Go for it!" Twilight said, "I trust you!"

Colt reached behind his belt and pulled out a swimming mask and a miniature flashlight. He climbed on top of the wooden guardrail and looked down. The silver water looked arctic cold. The height from which he was to jump from was even less appealing. There was no time to delay and he knew it. He strapped on his diving mask and turned on the flashlight.

"GERRONIMO-O-O-O-O!"

The water welcomed him with an icy squeeze.

CHAPTER 48

If one were to going to avoid crossing Donovan's Bridge by hobbling down one hill and then swim across Raven River, chances are he or she would be unsuccessful. Colt was aware of this. Going up the hill was dangerous as well, but Angel and Jadeite had no other choice. They made baby steps and leaned their weight forward. Thorn bushes with strong roots provided them with more support as they grabbed onto their vine-like stems. Though they were out of the freezing river, their teeth hadn't stopped chattering and climbing up the steep hill in their clinging heavy wet clothes made their struggle more difficult.

"Careful now, we're getting there," Jadeite said as he took another step upward.

"We gotta go faster," Angel said.

"We gotta stay focused," Jadeite said."One slip and we won't have to worry about Jack killing us."

Angel nodded. Her white mask felt like moss against her skin. She couldn't wait to take it off the first chance she got. Her bow and the few remaining arrows that didn't fall into the river had also tangled on many of the bushes. Any way she cut it, Angel knew that it was going to take more time than usual to get to the top of the hill on the Donovan's Grove side.

As Jadeite made another couple of steps, he looked up at Donovan's Bridge. Twilight and Jack's dark shapes were still battling.

Twilight was gaining the upper hand. The punches he had given Jack were starting to show as Jack's eyes swelled up. His face looked like an olive-green moldy prune. He tried to give Twilight one more punch. Twilight blocked it and flipped him to the planked floor.

"Like I said before: it's over, Jack," Twilight said. "I don't care how many pairs of handcuffs it takes."

"NEVER!" Jack said. He grabbed his lantern and swung with all his might. The lantern hit Twilight on the side of his rib cage. Twilight held onto his side and grunted.

"I know when I'm not wanted," Jack said.

He waddled toward the Sleepy Owl end of Donovan's Bridge. If he could make it to the forest, he could lose his adversaries—at least until the odds were in his favor. Twilight chased after him, though his battered body hurt with every step. Jack was closing in on the end of the bridge when a white horse came into view. Its forelegs jumped off the ground and kicked at the air as it neighed. Jack recoiled. The horse was Phantom and his rider was Moonbeam. Specter faded into view from the shadows in transparent form. She readied her purple wampum whip.

"End of the line, loser," Moonbeam said. He pointed his silver staff at Jack.

After diving into the river, Colt knew that the chances of finding the black box were as dim as the water around him. He was already twenty-five feet underwater and had at least another dozen feet to go before he reached the bottom. Each inch was getting colder and darker, but somehow, he held his breath well. It had only been thirty seconds since he jumped from the guardrail. He could probably go another minute if he had to, but it was hard to concentrate on finding the box as the temperature dropped.

Somehow, luck was in his favor. At the bottom of the river, was an old sign that said, "SLEEPY OWL: Population 3309. Established: 1690." The sign had been painted white. It stood out in the somber waters. On top of that sign was a stone that looked too square to be just another rock that local kids tossed into the river on their way to or from Donovan's Grove. Colt swam down to it and picked it up. The light from his miniature flashlight confirmed that it was the stone box that contained the burning red coal.

"Get your filly out of the way!" Jack said to Moonbeam. He made a swatting movement with his arm.

"I don't think so," Moonbeam said.

Jack knew that his lantern wouldn't work on any of them. As powerful as he was, he couldn't match strength with a stallion and two Pniese. His best bet now was to head back to the Donovan's Grove end of the bridge. He emit an angry shout and whirled around, his coat tails flapping behind him. Twilight was standing near the middle of the bridge, still holding onto his rib cage.

Moonbeam called out to Jack before he could get too far.

"I want to introduce you to a friend of mine," Moonbeam said. "Her name is Pandusa."

Phantom took one step to the side and revealed Pandusa who had been hiding behind him the whole time. She was no more than a yard tall, dressed in a light blue toga with snakes for hair. Her scaly skin almost had the same green tone as Jack's. Pandusa took off her sunglasses and revealed a set of glowing yellow eyes.

Jack felt his arms and legs stiffen. He screamed, but it was cut off as he morphed into a rough gray hue. With the exception of his lantern, Jack had changed into stone.

Twilight punched the air. "Yeah!"

"Is it done?" Moonbeam said.

Pandusa put her sunglasses back on. "Uh-huh."

"Good work," Moonbeam said. He felt for her shoulder and pet it.

Colt saw a blue-gloved hand extend to him when he almost reached the top of the steep hill on the Donovan's Grove side. Twilight stood in front of him and smiled. "Not bad."

Colt took hold of Twilight's hand and allowed his mentor to pull him up to the top. "Not bad. But not good either, right?"

"No," Twilight said. "Good. Real good." He put Colt in a playful headlock and gave him a noogie.

Colt couldn't help but grin, but it soon faded. He held up the stone box. "Here's the coal, let's get him!"

"Uh, that's not going to be necessary," Twilight said as they made their way back to the Donovan's Grove end of the bridge. Jadeite and Angel were there waiting, just as numb and soaked as Colt was.

"What do you mean that ain't gonna be necessary?" Colt said.

"Well, we found out that Jack isn't invincible," Twilight said. He pointed to the other side of the bridge. They saw the back of a stone statue. "Turns out that he's vulnerable when it comes to looking at gorgons."

"Aww man!" Colt said, "You mean to tell me that I went swimming for nothing?"

"I wouldn't say for nothing," Twilight said. "You certainly proved a lot to me."

"As well as the rest of us," Angel said. She gave Colt a wet hug.

"Yeah, yeah," Colt said. "I'm sure there could've been a better way without having to freeze my tail off."

Angel released her embrace, took the stone box, and started to walk across the bridge with Twilight.

Jadeite opened his arms to Colt. "Hug?"

"Up yours," Colt said.

Jadeite laughed as he and Colt followed behind Twilight and Angel.

CHAPTER 49

Jack was a stone statue. His mouth and eyes wide, recalling the last expression on his face before he met Pandusa. One hand was on his lantern near his stomach while the other was outstretched toward the Sleepy Owl end of the bridge as if he tried to stop the stone-changing process. On the Sleepy Owl side, Pandusa, Moonbeam, and Specter were standing by Phantom who was feeding on some grass.

Colt approached them. "I'm glad this night is over. "

"All the hard stuff is done," Specter said. "It's all sweet roses from here."

"What else have we got to do?"

"Oh, just one last patrol around town, then back to Huford House."

"So how do you think you did?" Moonbeam said to Colt.

"I think I'm smokin' hot," Colt said. "Actually, I wish I was smokin' hot instead of feeling like I've been hanging out at the North Pole."

"Moonbeam! Specter!" Angel said. She, Jadeite, and Twilight were still on the bridge behind Jack's stone body. "Go to Twilight's trunk and get some blankets before we catch our death of cold!"

Specter raised her hand. "Right!" She turned to Colt. "You got the keys, right?"

Colt nodded and reached into his frigid damp pocket. He pulled out the car keys and dropped them into to her palm.

As she and Moonbeam walked toward the car, Colt turned around and limped toward the Jack statue. His white slit eyes fixed onto Jack's rock eyes. Jack wasn't that big or smart and didn't have a diabolical plan to take over the world. Yet, he gave all six of them a run for their money. He beat both Colt and Twilight to a pulp. He nearly drowned Jadeite and a score of others. He shrugged off all the weapons that were used against him, but in the end, he lost. That made Colt smile and for a couple of seconds, he forgot how cold he was.

"That's right!" he said to the statue and poked it in its stony chest. "Maybe you'll think twice next time you come around here with an attitude! Next time, we'll really go medieval on you!"

"He can't hear you, Colt," Twilight said in the distance.

Colt peeked over Jack's shoulder and saw Twilight, Angel, and Jadeite. "I'm just saying it in case he can!"

There was a loud crack. Then a thundering explosion of pebbles and concrete.

The stone statue of Jack shattered. It was just a shell and the breathing Jack was underneath...and free once more.

He snatched Colt with his free arm and spun around, using the boy as a shield as he did with Moonbeam and Darby the leprechaun earlier in the evening. A few feet away, Angel whipped out her bow and reached for an arrow while Jadeite took out his slingshot. Jack held up his lantern to them, preventing them from stepping any closer.

"When are you cretins going to realize that nothing can bind me?"

"Leave the kid alone!" Angel said, "Tell us what you want!"

"What do I want?" Jack said as he tightened his grip around Colt's throat, "I want the human race to march into the shark-infested ocean, two by two, only to surface in little bloody pieces! I want to find acceptance in Heaven or with the Devil! But I can't have any of those, can I?"

"If you don't let that kid go," Twilight pointed at Jack, "I am personally gonna take that lantern and jam it right up your—!"

Angel slapped Twilight on the arm. "That's right," she muttered, "Let's piss him off a little more."

Jadeite wasn't listening to Angel or Twilight. He focused on Jack. This time, he was careful not to stare directly into the lantern. He only made a couple of glances as he shifted his eyes back and forth from Jack's face to the lantern. When he glanced back at the lantern, he noticed that the lantern's door was opening by itself.

He then turned his attention to Colt, who also noticed the lantern's door, now wide open. They nodded at each other while Jack was still addressing Angel and Twilight, preaching his rage and self-pity.

"Gimmee the coal," Jadeite whispered, holding out his green-gloved hand inches away from Angel's hip. "Quickly."

"…And for years, centuries even, I walked this wretched planet!" Jack said, "And what do they do? They named a vegetable after me!…"

"This guy has got serious issues," Twilight said to Angel.

"He's like that insane uncle everyone has in their family," she said and nonchalantly passed the stone box to Jadeite.

Jack was so indulged in his anger and list of demands that he didn't realize Jadeite had taken out the piece of burning red coal from the stone box and placed it in his slingshot's cradle.

"Now, Colt!" Jadeite said. He pulled back his slingshot's thick elastics.

Jack suddenly realized that the cursed coal was aimed at him. He felt a painful blow to his stomach as Colt elbowed himself free and dived to the bridge's planked floor.

Jadeite fired the coal.

It sailed across the bridge and punched into the opening of Jack's lantern.

The lantern's door swung shut by itself.

"NOOOOOOOOOOOOO!!" Jack said.

His lantern blinked with vibrant colors. Pink lightning surrounded and forked across his body. He twisted and vibrated as if he stuck his tongue in a bulb-less lamp. His orange eyes bulged to the point where it looked as if they were going to pop out of their sockets. They didn't. The pink lightning dissolved and left behind the sound of a few electrical snaps. The lantern that once shined turquoise light was now red again.

Jack looked different, somehow. He still had hatred in his eyes. His rotten teeth grind together as if he were trying to drive them further into his gums. Angel believed it was his posture. As she walked closer to him, she saw that he was slightly hunched over. His head was down. She picked up his ratty top hat.

"No." he said to himself. "No…I was free…I couldn't be captured… you can't bind me…no, no…" He shut his eyes tight. "Noooo!"

Angel handed him his hat. "See you later, Jack."

He swiped his hat and placed it on his head. "Kids. I always hated kids. Always messing things up! Couldn't just stay out of my affairs, could you?"

"My duty is to protect this town," Angel said. "You meddled in my affairs."

Jack opened his mouth, but no words came out. Instead, he just sneered.

Angel pointed to Donovan's Grove and beyond. "I believe you have some walking to do."

Just like that, Jack was gone.

He walked past her, Twilight, Jadeite, and made his way across Donovan's Bridge. His lantern's red light bobbed among the trees then disappeared into its shadows. Jack's feet made crunching sounds as they treaded on dry leaves and dead branches, but those noises soon drifted off as well until there was nothing but silence.

Moonbeam was handing out thick blankets. Jadeite and Colt had removed their drenched black sweatshirts and wrapped the soft quilts around their bare torsos. Angel put her arm around Jadeite and kissed his cheek.

"Good shot," she said. "You're going to be a good leader next year."

"You were a good leader this year," Jadeite said. "We've couldn't have done it without you."

"We couldn't have done it without all of you," Angel said as she looked around at everyone.

"There's just one thing I don't get," Colt said.

"What's that?" Twilight said.

"How did the door to Jack's lantern open and close all by itself?"

A tapping was heard.

At the edge of the bridge, Specter started to re-appear as she used her wampum whip as a jump rope. The tapping came whenever the center of the wampum whip hit the planked floor. Each time she skipped, she became more visible until she was as solid as the next person was. She leaned on the right post at the end of the guardrail.

"That would be my doing," she said.

Colt turned to Twilight. "Man, we need to get one of those things."

CHAPTER 50

Town square was almost empty by ten o'clock.

Pandusa and her family said their "good-byes" and left. Many volunteers for the annual Halloween party were going around with trash bags in hand, picking up used *Styrofoam* cups, dishes, plastic cutlery, napkins, and the black vinyl tablecloths that were used for the long buffet. Other volunteers stood on ladders and fumbled with taking the decorations from the trees down like the strings of saffron lights and the ghosts made from white sheets tied around softballs. Another volunteer took apples out of a tub of water they used earlier.

Up the street, rustling, banging, and several voices were heard coming from the old Meriweather house as townsfolk busied to put away many of the spooky exhibits and shut down all the electrical props.

By the gazebo, Spider Web had packed up their musical gear with help from the Pniese and Count Torlock. The supernatural rock group were usually the last ones to return to the Netherworld.

"You got it?" Jadeite said as he helped strap a drum onto Hermy's back.

"Yep, thanks fellas," the hunchback turned around and shook Jadeite's hand.

"Same time next year?" Lockjaw, the zombie bandleader said.

"Wouldn't be the same without you," Angel said.

They shook hands and Lockjaw hoisted up a base guitar case. He military saluted everyone. "Stay cool, guys and gals."

"You too," Twilight said.

The Pniese watched Spider Web carry their equipment and head out of town square to the nearest forest, which was a couple of yards away from the fire station up the street. Count Torlock arched his back and smiled at his allies, revealing his fangs.

"And then there was one," he said.

"Thanks for your help," Angel said, hugging him. "Take care of yourself."

"My pleasure," Torlock said and looked at Jadeite. "That woman in the butterfly costume. Any chance that I can get her number?"

Jadeite snickered. "Sorry."

"Ah, just as well," Torlock said. "After all, the Netherworld doesn't have *Verizon* or *AT&T*."

"There's always next year, dude," Jadeite said.

"Indeed there is," Torlock said and nodded to everyone. "Farewell, my friends."

When no townsfolk were looking, Torlock stretched out his black and white cape and changed into a bat. He chirped and flapped his wings, heading for the moon.

Angel waved "good-bye", then turned to Moonbeam and Specter.

"We'll meet you back at Huford House."

CHAPTER
51

Moonbeam and Specter got off of Phantom and guided him through a small section of the woods. They walked past the decrepit rowboat and followed Raven River until finally, they were at Lake Black Feather's shores.

Specter put her arms around the horse's thick neck and tugged him close to her.

Moonbeam stroked the stallion a final time. "See you next year, Phantom. Take good care of yourself until then."

Phantom neighed. He trotted toward the water. Moonbeam's gray-gloved hand glided across Phantom's back as the stallion drifted away. Silver water splashed and made huge ripples as Phantom galloped deeper into the lake. The water rose higher and higher and then, he was underwater as if the horse meant to drown himself. After a couple rounds of air bubbles, Lake Black Feather subsided to its previous tranquility. Specter took Moonbeam's arm. They cut through the forest and onto the trail that lead back to Huford House.

"I guess I'll see you around school tomorrow," Specter said.

"Actually, tomorrow is Saturday," Moonbeam said.

"Oh, yes. I forgot," Specter forced a quick laugh then covered her eyes. Dork, she thought. "You got plans over the weekend?"

"I got band practice and then I have to meet some friends about planning the November dance," he said. "How about yourself?"

"I'm busy," she said in a speed and in a way as if assuring him that she was. "Mary Anna and I have got a ton of things to do for the student council…Are you going to the dance with anyone?"

"Nah, I'll probably just collect the tickets and hang with the guys. Are you going to the dance?"

"Um, no. I'm not much of a dancer and I got a lot of studying to do."

"That's cool. They're not that great anyway, the dances. I'm just doing it as a favor for a buddy of mine."

"I think it just puts pressure on us," Specter said. "It's as if you're a loser if you don't bring someone to these things. It's all kind of shallow when you think about it."

"Yeah," said Moonbeam. "Well, I guess I'll see you around school Monday."

CHAPTER 52

"Relieved?" Twilight said as he and Colt went inside Huford House.

"Yeah," Colt said. "And no. It's strange, really. I'm cold, wet, and sore, and my knee is swelling up like a balloon. But…"

"But you feel strangely good at the same time," Twilight said.

"Yeah, I do."

"It happens to all of us. Don't ask me to explain it. I can't."

They made their way up to the second floor and into a bedroom that the boys had changed in earlier. The room was filled with a dirty orange hue because of all the lit candles. Bill Swifburg, formerly known as Jadeite, was already there as he pulled on his Sleepy Owl Tomahawks sweatshirt. Colt can tell from the light that Bill's hair was still wet. Nevertheless, the big guy smiled.

"Dude, I'm gonna take the longest, hottest shower when I get home," he said.

"That makes two of us," Colt said.

"Make it three," a female voice said from behind.

Twilight and Colt turned around. Bill looked over their shoulders. Cindy Daniels, formerly known as Angel, was by the doorframe. Her black and white costume, like Bill's black and green, were hung up in a hope chest, waiting to be filled again next year. Like Colt's and Bill's, her hair was still drenched from Raven River. She had put it up in a ponytail.

Colt took off his red, raccoon-style mask for the last time. White slits no longer represented his eyes. They were brown again. Willy Hynes was dying to get out of his black and red costume.

"Who's going to be the Colt next year?" he said.

"That's my responsibility," Cindy said. "Don't worry, I've got someone in mind."

"That means this outfit and the name of 'Twilight' is yours now," said Willy Hynes's former mentor.

Slowly, Twilight peeled off his blue, raccoon-style mask. Willy believed that Twilight was trying to savor every last second and in a way, he didn't blame him. The blue mask did come off and Vince Thomason was exposed.

He sighed. "Wow. That was tougher than I thought." He extended the mask to Willy Hynes.

Willy took the mask from the blue-gloved hand. "I'll wear it with honor, m' man. Then again, if I wear that outfit, I'll be fighting the bad guys with one hand and holding up my pants with the other."

"I'm sure there's something around here that's more your size," Vince said. He didn't realize that Willy was joking. The shock of no longer being a Pniese and in about two months, no longer being a teenager was setting in. Vince took off his cape. Willy did the same. They handed their silver badges to Cindy Daniels to put away.

"Well," said Bill Swifburg, "I'm gonna skedaddle before I miss the *Simpsons*."

"You're all done with everything?" Cindy said.

"Everything but scrubbing the latrine."

Cindy shook her head and chuckled through her nose as Bill walked past her. She soft-kicked his buttocks on his way out. She waved "goodbye" to Vince and Willy and left them to change.

As Willy gathered the clothes he wore during the day, Vince cupped his shoulder. He turned around and saw that Vince had a notebook and pen in hand.

"There's one more thing we need to take care of," Vince said.

"What's that?" Willy said.

Vince handed him the notebook and pen. "Paperwork. We have to write down all that happened tonight in case future Pniese members need to use our experience as references or creature identification."

Willy rolled his eyes. "Suddenly, swimming in the river doesn't seem so bad."

CHAPTER 53

November 3

Bus number four hissed as it came to a stop on Woodland Avenue. Hinges squealed as the bus driver pushed the lever that made the door fold. Willy Hynes stepped aboard with his Social Studies text and his book of stories by O. Henry.

The bus jerked as it pulled away. Willy staggered for an instant. He found a vacant seat towards the end of the back. That's where all the eighth-graders hung out on the bus. It was an unofficial rule that Willy suspected would follow him next year in high school. Freshmen would have to sit in the front, nerdy sophomores got the middle while the "in crowd" sophomores got the back along with the "non-in crowd" juniors. Willy theorized that "cool" juniors and seniors took their own car to school, at least his friend, Vince Thomason, did at sixteen.

He set his books down and cuddled up to the window. He stared at the post-Halloween environment. As they got to the end of Woodland Avenue, there was a smashed pumpkin on the street. Toilet paper hung from several trees and a set of power-lines. The houses that had been egged had been cleaned. When bus four stopped on Jenkins Avenue, Willy saw a car's windshield still covered in shaving cream. Some adults think that such acts are a sign of disrespect. For the young, however, it was good, clean fun. Willy always thought so. Then he wondered if Vince still thought that way and would his opinion change as he got older...as he headed into adulthood.

"Move your books, will ya?" Daryl Julson approached him.

He moved his books to his lap and allowed his friend to sit next to him. The same friend who was lucky to still be alive after crossing the thing called, "Jack."

"What's happening?" Daryl said, "You look a little bushed."

"Yeah, I am a little," Willy said.

"What a weekend I had," Daryl said. "Me and Bobby McHooley went out and did some serious tricking. We came across this guy dressed like a leprechaun and managed to sneak some of his gold away, at least we think it was gold. It sure looked a lot like it, but not really. It didn't have that plastic feel to it, you know?"

"Really?" Willy said, "I hope you had the brains to return it. Or did Bobby get you in trouble again?"

"That's a whole other story," Daryl said. "I know this sounds crazy, but I don't remember some things. I mean, on Halloween, me and Bobby were hanging out at Trevor Wallace Field and the next thing I know, I'm standing at the *7-Eleven* on Elm Street talking to this kid in a Dracula cape."

"Is that right?" Willy said.

"You think maybe I got a concussion or something?" Daryl said, "I heard you can have short-term memory loss after a concussion."

"You look fine to me. Did you tell your parents about it?"

"Yeah, my Dad asked me some questions like my birthday and address and what was on television a few minutes ago. He said that I was okay and told me to get some rest."

"Maybe next time you'll think twice before hanging out with Bobby McHooley again," Willy said.

"Well I tried calling you, but your mother said you had been gone all day with Vince," Daryl said. "What did you end up doing?"

THE END

COMING SOON…
HALLOWEEN NIGHT FEVER:
THE CIR-CUSS COMES TO TOWN
for more details, check out www.halloweennightfever.com

CPSIA information can be obtained
at www.ICGtesting.com
Printed in the USA
BVOW06s1938160117
R7781500001B/R77815PG473527BVX2B/1/P